THE "WITCH OF AVONLEA" MAKES AN APPEARANCE . . . IN CHURCH!

Peg Bowen's first step up the aisle sent a ripple of outrage through the congregation. Stirs, rustles, mumbles, and squeaks broke in every direction as Peg eyed the crowded pews. No one wanted a lost sheep anywhere in their personal vicinity.

"Spread out so she doesn't sit with us," Mrs. Biggins whispered hastily to her family. All of them immediately stuck out their elbows and spread out their coats so that not a spare inch was left in the Bigginses' pew.

"I can smell her from here," Mrs. Tarbush announced, loud enough to be heard halfway to the pulpit.

And Mrs. Sloane, who gave herself more airs than anybody, made no pretense at all about keeping her voice down. "Would you just look at that creature. If she sits here, I'm leaving."

Peg stopped dead in the middle of the church. She hitched up her knitted shawl and glared at several of the villagers in turn. Everyone sat stock-still as Peg's gaze raked over them, exposing their discomfort. Everyone, that is, save the one other uncertain new presence in the church. The only one, perhaps, who could understand Peg's situation.

"You can sit here, Miss Bowen," Peter Craig invited. Hetty gasped with outrage and Felicity looked as though she were going to faint. . . .

Also available in the Road to Avonlea series from Bantam Skylark Books

The Journey Begins
The Story Girl Earns Her Name
Song of the Night
The Materializing of Duncan McTavish
Quarantine at Alexander Abraham's

Conversions

Storybook written by
Gail Hamilton

Based on the Sullivan Films Production
written by Patricia Watson
adapted from the novels of

Lucy Maud Montgomery

A BANTAM SKYLARK BOOK
NEW YORK • TORONTO • LONDON • SYDNEY • AUCKLAND

Based on the Sullivan Films Production produced by Sullivan Films Inc. in association with CBC and the Disney Channel with the participation of Telefilm Canada adapted from Lucy Maud Montgomery's novels.

Teleplay written by Patricia Watson.

This edition contains the complete text of the original edition.
NOT ONE WORD HAS BEEN OMITTED.

RL 6, 008–012

CONVERSIONS

A Bantam Skylark Book / published by arrangement with HarperCollins Publishers Ltd.

PRINTING HISTORY
HarperCollins edition published 1991
Bantam edition / September 1992

Storybook written by Gail Hamilton.

For information address: HarperCollins Publishers Ltd., Suite 2900, Hazelton Lanes, 55 Avenue Road, Toronto, Canada M5R 3L2.

ISBN 0-553-48032-4

Bantam Books are published by Bantam Books, a division of Bantam Doubleday Dell Publishing Group, Inc. Its trademark, consisting of the words "Bantam Books" and the portrayal of a rooster, is Registered in U.S. Patent and Trademark Office and in other countries. Marca Registrada. Bantam Books, 666 Fifth Avenue, New York, New York 10103.

PRINTED IN THE UNITED STATES OF AMERICA

OPM 0 9 8 7 6 5 4 3 2

Chapter One

The kitchen of Rose Cottage was filled with tantalizing smells as Sara Stanley and her cousin, Felicity King, baked a marble cake to take to the church picnic. Sara had wanted to bake the cake by herself, but Felicity, who prided herself on being the best thirteen-year-old cook in Avonlea, didn't trust Sara to uphold the King family honor in matters culinary. She had marched over to supervise, and ended up taking over completely.

Felicity kept one eye anxiously on the oven while she wrestled with the knotty problem of what kind of icing to make. A cake for a church picnic was a tricky thing. On one hand, Felicity wanted the cake to be noticed. But on the other hand, she didn't want it to stand out so boldly as to have its maker tagged a show-off. Just the right note of tasteful, modest superiority was what she wanted to hit. Felicity cared a great deal about what Avonlea thought of her. To Felicity, appearances were everything.

She settled finally on straight chocolate. Her cake would be plain as a parson's coat on the outside—but inside, melting with sweet surprise. Now, the next most important matter was deciding how she herself should look.

"I'm not sure if I should wear my best or second-best dress to hear the visiting missionary," she said to Sara, determined to solve everything at one go.

If Felicity wore her best dress, the missionary might get an inflated idea of his own importance. However, if everyone else wore their best and Felicity found herself caught in only her second-best, she wouldn't be able to enjoy a single word of the sermon for worrying about her gaffe. In vain, Felicity looked to Sara for a sensible opinion on the matter.

Sara, blind to such social niceties, could think only about the exciting guest. The chance to hear a missionary who had actually been among the heathens was a rare thing in Avonlea, and she intended to squeeze every last drop of pleasure from the experience. Her imagination was already running away with her, anticipating all the hair-raising tales the visitor would tell. Cheering up the pews with a splash of brightness seemed the *least* she could do for a man who had slogged through the snake-infested tropics and lived to talk about it in the Avonlea church. She knew exactly what she was going to wear.

"I'm going to wear pink," she informed Felicity. "I want to cheer him up after all the horrible things he's been through in the jungle."

Peter Craig, Rose Cottage's hired boy, was also sitting in the kitchen. On impulse, Sara turned to speak to him.

"Peter, why don't you come to church with us on Sunday? There's going to be a wonderful picnic after," she added by way of extra enticement. Knowing Peter's weakness for cake, she glanced significantly towards the oven.

Peter sat in a far corner, ostensibly mending a bridle but, in reality, watching keenly everything that was going on. He especially liked to watch Felicity, though goodness knows why, for Felicity had a very low opinion of hired boys.

Peter was a stocky fellow barely older than Felicity, with his ankles and wrists showing rather prominently where he was growing out of his clothes. Under a thick sprinkling of freckles, he had a pleasant, slightly wary face. Shy brown eyes peered out from under a thatch of raggedly cut sandy hair that swept down over them. Peter always took an interest in what went on in the kitchen at Rose Cottage but, hungry lad though he was, not even Felicity's cake could tempt him near the Avonlea church. He ducked his head and shook it.

"Nah, I'm not going."

"Why not?" Sara instantly wanted to know.

Avonlea was a vigorously church-going community, and anyone who didn't do their Sunday duty was considered odd, if not downright suspicious. Peter knew he'd better have a good reason for not wanting to show up, especially with the added inducement of a missionary's adventures, and he came up with one fast.

"I'm not a Presbyterian."

In one stroke, Peter set himself against the common grain of society, for Avonlea was Presbyterian to its core. Too late, Peter realized that this rash admission was no way to gain points with Felicity.

"He's a heathen," Felicity put in haughtily. "Edward Ray even said he looks like a heathen."

Instantly, Peter flushed, not sure what heathens looked like but aware, in a most uncomfortable manner, that the cuffs of his overalls were frayed all round, and one elbow all but poked out of his shirt.

"I am not!" Peter burst out, hotly defending himself from both Felicity and the jibes of her swaggering schoolmate, Edward Ray. "I intend to be something some day, just like the rest of you. I just haven't decided what yet."

Unimpressed, Felicity started measuring out icing sugar.

"Well, deciding's not the same as being born something."

For Felicity, being born an Avonlea Presbyterian, and a King to boot, was a wonderful convenience. For the rest of her life, she felt, she'd never have to decide about anything more taxing than how big a cake to make or which of her dresses to wear. Her smug expression was finally too much for Sara, who chose that moment to fling herself into the argument.

"I think deciding what you'll be is a great deal better," she broke in, trying to rescue Peter and, at the same time, throwing herself wholeheartedly behind the exercise of free thought. Sara was a great advocate of free thought. Her Aunt Hetty, who was also the Avonlea schoolmistress, suspected that Sara indulged in the practice far too much, and regularly did her best to curb the dangerous habit.

Peter had by now given up altogether on the bridle he was supposed to be mending. He still had his eye on Felicity, who pointedly ignored him. When she had turned her back on him completely, he knew he had to say something, anything, to get her attention.

"I have a hankering to be a Methodist," he declared recklessly.

"A Methodist!"

If Peter had intended to shock Felicity, he'd certainly succeeded. She spilled icing sugar right over the edge of the bowl. From her voice, you'd have thought Methodists wore bones through their noses and stole sheep by the light of the moon.

"My aunt was a Methodist," Peter plunged on defiantly. Unlike Felicity, Peter had scarcely a relative to his name so he was willing to claim even such socially questionable ones as Methodists.

"What do you mean, she *was*?" Sara asked, wondering how much icing might be left in the bowl after Felicity was done.

"She's dead now." Peter paused, then wrinkled up his brow as though he had just thought of something. "Do you go on being a Methodist after you die?"

This question was too much even for Sara—and Sara was rarely short of an answer for anything. She looked across the table at Felicity, but all she got for her trouble was a disdainful shrug.

"I know one thing," Felicity rapped out, going at the icing ferociously with a wooden spoon. "I would rather be dead than be a Methodist!"

Sara's mouth popped open, but she managed to snap it shut again before any humorous comments jumped out of it. All she dared do was wait until Felicity looked away, and then she gave Peter a big grin. Peter, in spite of the drubbing he had just taken from Felicity, grinned back. He was not without a sense of perspective, and though being a Methodist might be drastic, it was not nearly as dreadful as the alternative Felicity had just advocated!

The day of the much-awaited church service and picnic finally arrived. While everyone else at Rose Cottage was in a flurry getting ready, Peter worked in the yard. He hadn't changed his mind, though he felt like the only person in Avonlea who wasn't on his way to church that day.

Hetty, Olivia and Sara, all gloriously arrayed in their Sunday finery, descended the front steps, and Peter glimpsed some of the splendor he was going to miss by stubbornly staying at home. Sara, with her pink muslin and her long blond hair, was pretty enough to cheer up a whole troop of missionaries, and her Aunt Olivia looked almost girlish in a yellow print dress. Even her Aunt Hetty, who was usually satisfied with a dark, tailored skirt and stiff white blouse, cut an impressive figure in rustling mauve serge and a new hat. Hetty, Olivia's older sister, was particular about her dignity, for besides being schoolmistress, she was the eldest of the King clan. She regarded herself as head of the family in particular and an uplifting example to the community in general. Though Sara had lived with her aunts in Avonlea only a short time, and it hadn't always been easy, she was beginning to think of Hetty as a second mother to her.

The three progressed grandly towards the horse and buggy. Peter had left it in readiness, with the mare tethered to the gate. He stood gazing at the spectacle until Sara spotted him and darted away from the group. At once, Peter looked away and applied himself energetically to the pump handle, filling the trough with water for the horses. He'd been very lucky to get this job with Hetty King, and he didn't want to be caught looking idle.

"Peter!" Sara cried. "Peter, I wish you would come with us. It's still not too late to change your mind. There's going to be ice cream and everything afterwards."

At the gate, Aunt Hetty was already climbing up into the buggy seat, and she twisted around in exasperation. Besides being a woman of strong opinion and firm command, Hetty was a stickler for punctuality.

"Sara Stanley, stop dilly-dallying. You're to leave Peter alone. We will be late for church."

The mention of ice cream had put a gleam of longing into Peter's eye, but Hetty's impatience promptly extinguished it. Stoutly, Peter thrust away this ready-made opportunity to flirt with Presbyterianism.

"Nah, I better not."

"Please," Sara begged. She hated to see anyone left behind when there was enjoyment afoot.

Peter only pumped harder, sending a torrent of water into the trough. Behind them, Olivia climbed up into the buggy beside Hetty. Olivia was much younger than Hetty, and as mild and pliant as her sister was angular and strong-willed. Everything ran smoothly at Rose Cottage as long as Olivia deferred to Hetty's authority.

"Sara," Olivia called out anxiously. Though she would never have let on to Hetty, Olivia was almost as excited as Sara about hearing the missionary, and she didn't want to be late.

Reluctantly, Sara walked back and climbed up behind her aunts. She might have failed to persuade Peter this time, but Sara was not one to give up easily once she had set her heart on a project. Next Sunday, she resolved, Peter would go with them to church, even if it *was* Presbyterian.

Olivia, who got along with horses a whole lot better than Hetty, gave the reins a shake. Blackie, their mare, started out down the road. They'd got no further than a few yards, however, when they were startled by a strange apparition stumping across their own front pasture.

"Stop the buggy!" Hetty commanded.

Flustered, Olivia hauled on the reins. "Whoa!"

Blackie, who had just got going nicely, halted grudgingly, for she was in the mood for a good, brisk trot. She now tried to crop at some clover by the roadside while waiting to start up again.

Hetty eyed the rapidly approaching figure,

which was recognizable even at a distance as Peg Bowen, known as the "witch of Avonlea."

"The nerve of that woman! When will that lunatic vagrant get it through her head she's not wanted around here?" Hetty half rose in the buggy seat and used her most commanding schoolmistress voice, which traveled great distances to piercing effect. "Here! You! Where do you think you're going?"

Peg gave no sign of hearing, though her ears were as good as those of any lynx. She wore two skirts flapping about her ankles and a man's baggy tweed jacket, patched in green at the elbows. The jacket was boldly topped by a red tartan shawl, and a brimmed, sea-going hat crushed down over one of Peg's bright black eyes. With everything blowing in the breeze, she looked like a pirate ship bouncing jauntily along with all sails set. And she never wavered once in her course across the field.

Blackie began to shake her harness impatiently, for Olivia had prevented her from getting at the clover.

"Now, Hetty, I'm sure she's just taking a shortcut," Olivia muttered, worried about how much longer Blackie could be trusted to stand still.

"She has no business trespassing."

Hetty was bristling all over at the very sight of Peg. If being a Methodist was radical in Avonlea, being a witch was beyond imagination. But Peg didn't care a fig for what Hetty or anyone else in Avonlea thought of her. She was a true eccentric; she had dared cut herself loose from all of society's rules and found the freedom delightful. Peg did what she liked, said what she liked and went wherever the spirit moved her. In summer, she lived practically wild in the fields. In winter, she snuggled up in a mossy, disreputable old cabin, snug from the blizzards and the snow. As a consequence of declaring her independence in so shocking a fashion, grown-ups chased Peg off whenever they saw her, children blanched at the mere glimpse of her skirts and the most fantastic tales circulated about her witchy powers.

Blackie snorted and began to sidle sideways, leaving Olivia in danger of losing the wrestling match with the reins.

"What do you think she's going to do? Put a hex on the hens?" Olivia grumbled to Hetty. "Gee-up," she told Blackie.

Since Blackie, quite fed up, had already begun to move off at a trot, the command served only to spare Olivia some embarrassment.

Peg gave the buggy a glance over her shoulder

and chuckled as it passed out of sight. Hetty King could shout at her all she liked, but it wouldn't do the least bit of good. Peg Bowen was not going to be intimidated by anyone in Avonlea, from Hetty King on down.

Chapter Two

The church service proved enthralling, quite living up to Sara's high expectations. Everyone who could possibly squeeze in was at church that morning. Every pew was full. Latecomers received disapproving stares as they straggled in and tried to find places to sit. Sara and her aunts, who, thanks to Blackie, had arrived in good time after all, sat right at the front in the King family pew. The rest of the family—Aunt Janet, Uncle Alec and their three children, Felicity, Felix and Cecily—were already there. Felix sat swinging his heels, for once actually wanting a church service to begin. Cecily, the youngest of Sara's cousins, kept craning her neck to see if the missionary would really show up in beads and hides as she had secretly supposed.

Sara was scarcely able to contain herself during the opening hymn and prayers, but now, at last, she gazed up in rapture at the main attraction. Reverend Brinsmead had taken full possession of the pulpit to hold forth upon his wild adventures among the unconverted. He talked about the stormy ocean voyage, the blistering heat, the lurking crocodiles. Slowly, with excruciating suspense, he described the journey of his intrepid little band as they hacked their way through miles and miles of trackless jungle, wondering whether they'd ever see another human face again.

"There we were..." He leaned forward, seeming to fix each listener with his burning eye, "...lost in the jungle, miles from civilization, when suddenly, we heard a blood-curdling shriek!"

For all that he was elderly and white-haired and looked as though he might collapse before even a medium-sized shriek, the Reverend Brinsmead knew how to hold an audience. All the King children sat wide-eyed and open-mouthed—even Felicity, who never hesitated to tell others they shouldn't make traps to catch flies.

"Next thing we knew," the Reverend Brinsmead continued, after a dramatic pause, "we were surrounded by natives wearing grass skirts and feathers, waving their spears about, their faces painted in the most horrible, blood-red patterns. They dragged us off to a village, where they had a huge, black cauldron of water over the fire, big enough for a man. 'Cannibals,' I thought. 'Only a miracle can save us now.'"

Felix looked as though he might expire from suspense, even though the missionary obviously did get saved, or he wouldn't have been standing there in the Avonlea pulpit. Of course, a miracle did save him. One of the missionaries had learned the language of the cannibals, and convinced them that they were good men, men of God. Soon, the heathens were friends, and the missionaries were able to bring them the word of the church. Needless to say, it could never have happened without the faith of all the good people back home who had contributed to the expedition. Missionaries never visited village churches without being on the lookout for donations toward their next brush with the cannibals' luncheon menu.

When the gripping account had finally ended, the congregation happily adjourned outside for the picnic. Sara and Felicity sat on a blanket with ten-year-old Cecily, who had been ordered to stay firmly under Felicity's eye. Though her blond hair often made Cecily look like a little angel, she was more than capable of getting up to mischief. Felix, who, at eleven, was in the middle between Felicity and Cecily, dashed straight to the tables laden with food and came back balancing a plate heaped with everything he could possibly get onto it.

Felicity, even in her second-best blue organdy, had found herself much more captivated by their visitor than she had expected to be.

"Wasn't that man interesting?" she said, tucking her skirt out of harm's way. "Cecily, eat your salad."

Cecily hated salads and, even more, hated being told to eat them. She poked glumly at the heap of green Felicity had piled onto her plate. Sara, almost too excited to eat, gazed mistily at a neighboring woodlot as though hoping painted savages would erupt from it even as she watched.

"The missionary field sounds so romantic," she sighed ecstatically. Sara was prone to getting carried away by farfetched notions. She saw herself for a moment as a heroine, slashing her way though vines and creepers with a whole train of devoted followers struggling in her wake.

"Being eaten by cannibals doesn't sound so romantic to me," Felix put in as he tried to sit down without spilling any ham rolls from his plate. His bald logic punctured Sara's daydream and made Felicity giggle.

"Well, I'm sure cannibals would just love to eat you, Felix," Felicity teased. Felix was temptingly plump and would have been the first morsel the cannibals served up.

"I'm sure they would. But, thank goodness, there are no cannibals in Avonlea."

Complacently, Felix slid his plate onto his knee, pulled a fork from his back pocket and set about demolishing a mound of potato salad. He meant to clean up everything in time to get a chance at Felicity's cake, which he knew would be as sweet as his sister was sour. He forgot about Sara, who was just then thinking that people didn't exactly have to boil Presbyterians in cauldrons to be in need of missionary attention. Enthusiasm flooded back into her face. She whipped her gaze from the woods and fixed it on Felix.

"No, there are no cannibals, but you can be a missionary right here in Avonlea. There are lots of folks who don't come to church."

Felicity all but choked on a mouthful of creamed peas. She turned sharply to her cousin.

"Sara Stanley, I know exactly what you are thinking, and I will not have that heathen, Peter

Craig, sitting in the same pew with me!" She spied Cecily quietly ditching pieces of cucumber into the long grass. "Honestly, Cecily, I told you to eat your salad!"

Despite Felicity's scorn, Sara had somehow managed to pick up the very thoughts that were running through the mind of Reverend Brinsmead on that sunny day, warm enough, perhaps, to remind him of his own jungle adventures. Once a missionary, always a missionary. Even in Avonlea, the good man could not restrain himself. As a small, admiring crowd gathered around him, he began to speak.

"The world is full of people in need, not only in the missionary field, but right here in Avonlea—people who are poor and lonely, who don't belong to the church. I want you to go out and find them, bring them to me."

Reverend Brinsmead began to get carried away with his own fervor. He waved one hand in the air while trying to hold onto a plate of diced carrots and cabbage rolls with the other. His sonorous plea reached the ears of Olivia, Hetty and Alec, who were making their way to a picnic table.

"I hope he knows what he's doing," Olivia said worriedly. Lines of religion were very settled in Avonlea. Reverend Brinsmead had no idea of the trouble his innocent words might stir up should anyone take them seriously.

Hetty jerked her head in agreement, foreseeing, as usual, only calamity.

"Lord knows what kind of riff-raff that kind of talk will bring in!"

Hetty set her jaw, clearly hinting that certain people had their place and ought to stay in it, and not think of storming Presbyterian strongholds. Her brother Alec, who tended to be an infuriatingly tolerant, easygoing man, laughed aloud at the notion.

"Oh, I don't know," he said, looking around at all the prim, respectable hats and men stiff inside their Sunday collars. "This church could do with a little shaking up."

Perhaps more than anyone else at the picnic, Sara had taken the missionary's rousing exhortation quite to heart. She had her own 'shaking up' in mind, and as soon as she got back to Rose Cottage, she went to work on the nearest candidate she could find—Peter Craig. Sara tracked Peter down in the barn, where she found him sitting on the milking stool, milking the jersey cow. After regaling Peter with a description of every single thing that had happened, Sara leaned against the post behind him, her eyes starry with memories of the day.

"You should have come with us, Peter. It was so exciting. Church is where everyone meets in Avonlea. Don't you ever want to come?"

Sara had a knack for description, and she had just made the church service sound like a whole day at the county fair. Peter leaned his forehead against the warm side of the cow, not wanting Sara to see his interest.

"I still haven't decided yet what I want to be—Presbyterian or Methodist," Peter mumbled recalcitrantly.

Reverend Brinsmead's sermon had put Sara far beyond petty theological hair-splitting. She dismissed Peter's objection with a wave of her hand.

"I really don't think there's much difference. And besides, there is no Methodist church in Avonlea."

To Sara, this was the clinching argument in favor of trying out Presbyterianism. Peter continued milking in silence for a moment, the milk sizzling into the pan in swift, frothy bursts. Then he peeped sideways at Sara.

"Why is it so important to you that I go? I'm

not like the rest of the people in this town."

Peter did such a good job of sounding casual that even Sara was fooled. The matter was hardly casual to Peter, though. Not only had he not been raised in Avonlea, he had had to come there as a hired boy because his own mother couldn't support him and his father was, well...out of the picture for a while, that was for sure. Jack Craig was in jail, and certain people in the neighborhood wouldn't let Peter forget it. Judging from the twist of his mouth, Peter might have suffered from this more than he was letting on. Sara, who hadn't been in Avonlea so long herself, only tossed her head airily.

"Don't be silly. Of course you are. Everyone wants to belong."

Peter didn't need to be told this as he poured the milk into the milk can and fed the purring barn cats. After all, it hadn't been much fun staying behind to muck out stalls while everyone else was hearing about jungle tribes and stuffing themselves with Felicity's marble cake.

Peter let the cow out into the barnyard and then sat down in the stable doorway, where the last rays of sun slanted warmly in. First he chewed on a piece of straw, then he poked at a knot in the door frame, and then he nibbled on the corner of his lip. Peter wanted to belong very much indeed, but there were obstacles.

"Well, anyway, I don't have Sunday clothes like the rest of you."

So! There it was—the real root of the debate about which kind of church Peter would favor. Sara let out a laugh of relief.

"Peter, is that all you're worried about? Why didn't you say so?"

Peter didn't answer that. A fellow had his pride, even if he was just a hired boy lucky even to have clothes to work in, never mind a fancy Sunday suit. It was only because Sara noticed him and stood up for him when she could that Peter had got up the courage to blurt out as much as he did. He didn't know whether to feel nervous or reassured about the way Sara was beaming back at him. When Sara Stanley decided to put a matter right, it was often advisable to take cover. Sara Stanley had been known to resort to some pretty odd solutions in her time.

Pleased that she now had a nice, solid problem to work on, Sara set about tackling it that very evening in the Rose Cottage parlor. Aunt Hetty had settled down to an edifying work of literature, while Olivia finished yet another square of the immense afghan she had been knitting for weeks. She held up the square in the yellow lamplight and admired the handiwork.

"This really is the most handsome afghan I've ever made for the mission, if I do say so myself. I'm sure it will keep some poor soul very cozy."

Hetty spared the square an absentminded glance. "Hmm, good. Haven't the patience for it myself."

Sara entered carrying a tray laden with a tea service, two cups of tea and a plate of ginger cookies. She had folded the napkins into little fans and used the tea set with the rosebud pattern. Sara Stanley knew how to set a stage when she needed to.

"Time for tea," she announced cheerily, peering at her aunts to measure their mood. When a girl was going to ask a favor, timing was everything.

Hetty looked up with pleased surprise. She had just been thinking about having a little refreshment.

"Why, Sara, how very thoughtful of you."

Sara saw both ladies well furnished with tea and cookies before she sat down and primly crossed her ankles. When she saw her Aunt Hetty taking a long, pleasurable sip from her cup, Sara launched slantwise into her main topic.

"Aunt Hetty, I've been thinking a lot about what Reverend Brinsmead said. Don't you think Peter should come to church with us?"

"He really should, Hetty," added Olivia, coming to Sara's support as she so very often did. "If he's living under our roof, I think it's our duty."

Hetty finished off a ginger cookie with a decisive crunch and dusted the crumbs away with her napkin. As a self-appointed moral leader in Avonlea, Hetty could hardly say that Peter should stay behind slaving in the fields when the family went to church. Nonetheless, Hetty felt that what hired boys did about religion was entirely their own concern.

"He will go if he wants to."

Sara saw that this was all the opening she was likely to get, so she had better make the best of it.

"Oh, he wants to. It's just...he doesn't have any Sunday clothes."

If Sara expected her Aunt Hetty to be moved by this revelation, she was fooling herself heartily. Hetty pulled her mouth into a tight, disapproving line that even ginger cookies couldn't improve.

"Humph! It's not my responsibility. The boy barely earns his keep as it is."

Peter had been taken on to replace Old Jake, who had kept the farm running smoothly for many years, right up until he had died. Peter hadn't been on the job very long, but already the difference was showing. Now Hetty, in a less than generous mood, began to list in her head all the chores Peter had not managed to get done.

"We send clothes to the mission field," Sara pointed out. She didn't quite dare to say that perhaps some mission work could be done right here in their own home.

"Used clothing," Hetty sniffed, as though only feathered tribesmen could wear the cast-off shirts of Avonlea.

Sara turned to Olivia. "Your afghan is new."

Hetty didn't take well to contradiction, especially from twelve-year-old girls. Her head came round sharply.

"Now you watch your step, Sara. I have no use for people who think church is simply a place to show off frills and fancy new clothes—that's for certain. If Peter really wants to go to church, he'll go. Nothing will stop him."

Hetty put aside her cup and picked up her book again, indicating that the conversation was over. Even though she herself had bought a new hat and insisted on her best mauve serge for the service and picnic, Hetty made it clear that she had little sympathy for a boy weak enough to let frayed trousers stand between himself and Presbyterian salvation.

Chapter Three

Reverend Brinsmead accepted an invitation from Reverend Leonard, Avonlea's regular minister, to visit at the rectory and speak to the congregation again the following Sunday. He stayed on for some days in Avonlea, enjoying the quiet of the rural village. No doubt he found it a restful change from screeching jungles, where one might be dragged off into the underbrush at any moment by annoyed panthers or cannibals planning a feast. Yet even in Avonlea, Reverend Brinsmead could not give up the missionary habit. Consequently, he made it a habit to stroll down Avonlea's main street with one eye open for possible converts.

It was while he was engaged in this kindly pursuit one day that he noticed something odd. As he walked down the street, he saw people becoming agitated, whispering to one another, gesturing towards someone he didn't recognize and making a show of crossing the street to avoid her. Surely, she made an odd-looking figure. Reverend Brinsmead's curiosity was piqued.

But even when a boy hissed, "Look, there goes the witch of Avonlea!" and dashed for cover in the general store, Reverend Brinsmead didn't catch on. He kept on walking, straight towards the strange personage the residents of Avonlea were so energetically trying to avoid—none other than Peg Bowen.

Perhaps, after gaudy chieftains and whooping tribesmen, Peg could hold no terrors for him. As if nothing were out of the ordinary, he kept right on through town until he all but bumped into Peg at the entrance to the covered bridge. Peg, who admired his gumption, paused in her path and, quite civilly, bid him good day.

This was opening enough for the minister. He came to a halt and extended his hand, exactly as though Peg were not wearing two skirts and a hat that looked as though it had been around the South Seas all on its own before taking up a battered retirement on her head.

"Good day. Have I had the pleasure of meeting you before?"

At this mild question, Peg took in the clerical collar and let out a snort of derision. Witches and

Christians had had a pretty uneasy history together, with the witches generally getting the worst of the bargain.

"Not likely," she growled. "But you might have heard about me. I'm Peg Bowen."

Reverend Brinsmead couldn't say that he had. To make up for the lack, he shook Peg's hand vigorously and bobbed his silver head again.

"Well, I'm most pleased to meet you. I'm Reverend Brinsmead. I hope you will join the Avonlea congregation to hear the second part of my lecture this Sunday."

It must have been a long time indeed since anyone had made such a proposal to Peg. Her eyebrows shot up and her lip stuck out and sparks flashed in her eyes.

"I ain't one of your flock, Reverend. I belong to the round church. The devil won't catch me lurkin' in the corners. Oh, no. I do my praying to God in the woods, amidst the flowers and the creatures of the field."

No doubt Reverend Brinsmead was used to dealing with stranger practices than this. Compared to cannibal philosophies, Peg's belief sounded more than sweetly reasonable, and Reverend Brinsmead wasn't one of those who would try to restrict all praying to inside the church. Nevertheless, he truly believed that the church had something to offer Peg that the woods could not. He also knew just what approach to take with the stubborn in his flock. He smiled all the more pleasantly at Peg.

"Well, we're all God's creatures. But we're human creatures, too. We need the friendship of our own kind. The Avonlea congregation would be delighted if you would participate at our Sunday meeting. Please say you'll come, Miss Bowen."

Several of the Avonlea congregation would have fainted dead away had they heard the good Reverend so cavalierly extending the hospitality of their church to one as wild and woolly as Peg Bowen. Peg knew this very well, and an expression of wry humor leaped into her sunburnt face. Humor—and something else, for Reverend Brinsmead was wise in the ways of common humanity. He had hit upon exactly the appeal Sara had used with Peter. It was a fine thing to live alone and free in the woods, as Peg had chosen to. But as she sat out howling blizzards and long black nights, Peg sometimes must have thought how nice it would have been to have friendship by her fireside. Now and then, even the wildest have a yen for the company of their own kind.

Before Peg could answer, a boy on a bicycle came thumping over the uneven planks of the bridge.

"Watch out she don't put a spell on you, Reverend," he called out as his bicycle whirred past. And he grinned nastily at Peg, who had to jump out of his way.

Peg glowered after the culprit, instantly revising the good opinion of humanity Reverend Brinsmead had been trying to instill.

"Human creatures they might be," she muttered dourly, "but friends, I'm not so sure of."

Reverend Brinsmead was once again to be the main attraction at church on the following Sunday, and at Rose Cottage, Sara felt her own heart beating with excitement at the prospect. Still determined to cheer the missionary, she had chosen her sunny yellow muslin, which had real lace down the tucks in front and the most elegant smocking along the yoke. The effect was so uplifting that Sara grinned at herself in the mirror, took a forbidden bounce on the bed for good measure and almost flew down the stairs. When she got to the front hall, she hastily composed herself, looked around, then called up the stairs behind her. She had something else to be excited about today. Like Reverend Brinsmead, she had prevailed upon a stubborn free thinker to consider the merits of church-going.

"Peter, are you ready?"

There was a long silence, then Peter's muffled voice.

"I'm not going."

Sara gave an exasperated sigh and set her lips. She had just spent a whole week exercising her considerable powers of persuasion on Peter. She wasn't going to let all that work come to nothing this close to the service.

"Peter Craig, come down here this minute!"

When she chose to, Sara could sound very compelling indeed. There was another silence, then Peter appeared on the landing. His young face was folded into a troubled frown.

"I'll be the only one with patches on my trousers."

"God won't notice," Sara assured him firmly.

"But the rest of Avonlea will."

And the rest of Avonlea intimidated Peter far more than God. However, before he could retreat, Sara dashed up to the landing again and inspected him up and down. Since new clothes hadn't been forthcoming from Aunt Hetty, Sara had decided that Peter must make do with what he had. Now even she was a bit taken aback by how scanty his Sunday wardrobe was.

"You have holes in your stockings. Don't you have another pair?"

"They have holes in them too."

Sara would not be defeated by two pairs of unmended stockings. She had got Peter this far, and she had to think fast.

"Well, maybe if you wear one pair on top of the other, then the holes won't show."

"Won't they look funny?" Peter wondered skeptically, admiring Sara for her ingenuity nevertheless.

"No, silly. Just do it, and hurry. We're late as it is."

Instead of moving, Peter hovered at the top of the stairs. He took in Sara's fine yellow dress with its real lace and fashionable rows of tucks. She looked such a fine young lady that he just knew he'd feel like a clod, trailing into church behind her in his rough, patched clothes. He hung his head and began to tug distractedly at one of the buttons on his shirt. Indeed, he began to look so uncertain about the whole church-going venture that Sara saw he was going to bolt altogether if she didn't do something drastic to keep his spirits up. If fancy dresses were the problem, then fancy dresses could be changed.

"Don't worry, Peter. You won't have to go through this alone," Sara assured him, as she started back towards her own room.

Outside, Hetty and Olivia waited restlessly in the buggy while Blackie tried her best to get at the flowerbeds.

"What are those children up to?" muttered Hetty, as Olivia jerked Blackie's head away from Hetty's prize zinnias. "Sara! Peter!"

The front door opened. Out came the two children. The smile on Hetty's face froze even before Peter and Sara got as far as the porch steps.

"Sara Stanley, what—? Have you completely lost your senses?"

Gone was the sunny yellow muslin and the brushed, loosened glory of Sara's curls. She was now encased in plain, navy wool with dark stockings and heavy, brown shoes, an outfit she kept to wear to school on the wettest, muddiest days. Her hair was pulled back in tight braids that disappeared down her back and left her face a scrubbed, oval expanse of earnestness and enormous eyes. Sara was expressing her solidarity with Peter in the most direct and obvious way she could think of.

"Aunt Hetty, you did say yourself that we don't go to church to show off our fancy clothes," Sara answered calmly, folding her hands together and continuing towards the buggy.

Hetty was caught out cold on a point of logic, and she knew it. Now she could do nothing but sit with her mouth open and a half-formed retort stuck in her throat. She closed her mouth and sniffed loudly instead.

"Once that child puts her hand to the plough," she muttered stiffly to Olivia, "there's no turning back. Well, it's too late to change now."

Exchanging a glance of secret victory, Sara and Peter climbed up into the buggy behind the two women. Blackie reluctantly gave up on the flowerbed to head for church.

Chapter Four

When the buggy from Rose Cottage arrived, its occupants descended briskly and approached the church in tight formation. Reverend Leonard greeted the congregation at the door. At his side, Reverend Brinsmead stood beaming, his eyes already bright with thoughts of the rousing speech he was preparing to deliver. Aunt Hetty, determined to do her duty, pushed Peter forward.

"Reverend Brinsmead, Reverend Leonard, this is Peter Craig, our hired hand. He's decided to join the congregation."

Reverend Leonard shook Peter's hand warmly, not at all prejudiced, it seemed, by patched trousers and two pairs of socks trying to conceal their holes.

"Welcome. Welcome to the fold."

Struck speechless by such a close encounter with a minister, Peter could do no more than bob his head awkwardly, before the crush of new arrivals pushed Hetty and her party onward into the church. As the minister turned his attention to those coming up behind him, Peter gaped at the gleaming, white-painted interior of the Avonlea church. He finally had to be given a sharp prod by Hetty towards the King pew.

Felicity, Felix and Cecily were already seated with their parents. The two younger Kings were having a hard time keeping still, despite the solemnity of the organ, which had been playing softly for some time in a somewhat vain attempt to put people into a religious mood.

Felix twitched his nose at the sight of Peter. Felicity stared in open dismay. Not only was she going to have to sit with a scruffy hired boy, but with a cousin who must have lost her senses entirely to come to church dressed like a field hand.

Her mouth set in a grim line, Hetty herded her charges into the pew and sat down on the far end, as though she were afraid Peter or Sara might escape and embarrass her further. When everyone was finally still, Uncle Alec leaned over to Peter.

"Peter, have you brought anything to put into the collection plate?" he asked quietly.

The matter of patched trousers had so absorbed Peter that he had forgotten all about other practical considerations. Now he had run smack up against a hard religious fact. Whether he chose to be a Methodist, a Presbyterian or a whirling dervish, it was still going to require money.

"No, I forgot, sir," Peter admitted in the midst of a fresh wave of panic. His ears began to turn a throbbing scarlet. In truth, most of what Peter earned he sent to his mother, and he hadn't any spare coins to lavish upon theology.

With a wink, Alec slipped a penny into Peter's hand.

"Here, take this."

There was no point in letting a hard encounter with economics scare off a fledgling Presbyterian his first time at a service.

"Doesn't he know anything?" Felix scoffed, catching sight of the exchange. Felix was made to earn his own pennies to put in the collection plate, and he resented Peter acquiring his offering so easily.

"Shh," his father warned sharply.

Before Felix could even make a face at Peter, both were distracted by a commotion at the back of the church. As Reverend Brinsmead was chatting with the last of the stragglers and Reverend Leonard was getting ready to close the doors, a startling vision swept through the church entrance. The congregation took a single look and gasped, from one end of the church to the other.

Peg Bowen!

Peg had apparently taken Reverend Brinsmead's words to heart and decided to give conventional society one more try. In honor of the occasion, she had shed her man's coat and one of her two skirts. The sea-going hat had been replaced by a shocking old straw bonnet, jauntily twined round with wildflowers from the church garden.

The congregation buzzed like a hive of angry

bees, but Reverend Brinsmead remained oblivious to their indignation. At the sight of Peg, his face lit up as though a cannibal chief had stepped down from his throne and condescended to hear a sermon.

"Miss Bowen, you've come!" he exclaimed. He immediately thrust out his hand in happy greeting.

Peg gave his hand a shake and took a few more steps into the church. Her snapping black eyes took wary measure of the interior.

"Years ago, I swore I would never darken these doors again. But you got me thinkin', Reverend. Maybe I've been missin' somethin'."

At this admission, Reverend Brinsmead swelled up as though he had just received a medal from the King himself. After years of effort under the tropical sun, he could be forgiven a little vanity about his own powers of persuasion. Giving way to a weakness for drama, he took Peg by the hand and led her down the central aisle.

"'What man of you, having an hundred sheep, if he loses one of them, doth not leave the ninety and nine in the wilderness, and go after that which is lost, until he find it?'"

The missionary meant well, but Peg's brows flew together at the sonorous biblical quotation.

She regarded her presence here as doing Reverend Brinsmead a favor and not the other way round. On top of that, she was mighty touchy about being labeled a lost sheep. If the Reverend needed live people to illustrate his sermons, Peg could see plenty of material seated right under his nose.

Still pleased with himself and missing the meaning of Peg's expression, Reverend Brinsmead again bade her welcome and released her to make her way up the aisle in search of a place to sit.

Peg's first step sent another ripple of outrage through the congregation. Stirs, rustles, numbles and squeaks broke in every direction as Peg eyed the crowded pews. No one wanted a lost sheep anywhere in their personal vicinity.

"Spread out so she doesn't sit with us," Mrs. Biggins whispered hastily to her family. All of them immediately stuck out their elbows and spread out their coats so that not a spare inch was left in the Biggins' pew.

"I can smell her from here," Mrs. Tarbush announced, loud enough to be heard halfway to the pulpit.

And Mrs. Sloane, who gave herself more airs than anybody, made no pretense at all about keeping her voice down.

"Would you just look at that creature," she cried. "If she sits here, I'm leaving."

This last was just too much for Peg. It had been displays of this sort of fine Christian spirit that had kept her clear of the Avonlea church and Avonlea society for so many years. Peg had just about no tolerance at all for hypocrisy, and she had a tongue that was a match for anyone.

"Don't worry," she shot at Mrs. Sloane. "I don't want to sit with any of you any more than you want to sit with me."

Mrs. Sloane's eyes bulged and she tossed her head indignantly. Peg had now stopped dead in the middle of the church. She hitched up her knitted shawl and glared at several of the villagers by turns. Everyone sat stock still as Peg's gaze raked over them, exposing their discomfort. Everyone, that is, save the one other uncertain new presence in the church. The only one, perhaps, who could understand Peg's situation.

"You can sit here, Miss Bowen," Peter invited, speaking up bravely when everyone else sat in frozen silence. Perhaps he didn't want to be left on his own as the only raw recruit in the church.

As Hetty gasped with outrage and Felicity looked as though she were going to faint, Peg swung round in surprise.

"Why, Peter! I didn't expect to see you with this two-faced lot." And before Peter even had a chance to look startled, Peg barreled on. "You're too good for the likes of these folks. Take Stephen Grant, for instance." She turned pointedly to a fat, prosperous, well-dressed man, "Look at him sitting there as if butter wouldn't melt in his mouth. He set fire to his house to get the insurance, and then he blamed me for it."

"Well, I never!" exploded Mrs. Sloane, even as the unfortunate Stephen Grant began to turn as red as though he had suddenly been set on fire himself.

"And Fanny Tarbush can give herself airs, but she's got nothing more holy on her mind than catching a rich husband."

"Have you ever *heard* such a thing?" choked out Mrs. Tarbush, looking as though she might faint and sink behind the back of the pew.

With a few well-placed darts, Peg had just proven she could give as good as she got. And she'd had plenty of practice. One of the great compensations for being called a witch was the pleasure of saying exactly what she liked, whenever she felt the need.

Peg walked up to the front of the church and

turned to the whole congregation.

"Why, I haven't missed a thing. Same old bunch of hypocrites, just a little older, that's all." She turned to smile at Peter and caught sight of Hetty, glaring fit to crack the window panes. Peg glared right back.

"I could tell a few stories about Hetty King," she drawled meaningfully.

Hetty jumped to her feet, her face as white as her best linen sheets. She couldn't remember when anyone had last dared to address her with such boldness. Since no one else seemed able to move, she decided to take charge of the situation herself.

"Peg Bowen, since you clearly have no respect for the sanctity of the church, I would ask you to leave just as fast as your wagging tongue will take you!"

It took a strong spirit not to quail before Hetty King, but Peg only stamped her foot.

"You should learn the true meaning of Christian charity, Hetty King," she flung back, undaunted.

Hetty's jaw hung open, but nothing more came out of it. She just stood there, looking like a wet cat. Beside her, Olivia and Alec's faces were flushed, but it was from a heroic attempt to squelch their amusement at seeing someone publicly stand up to their sister.

Peg took a step closer. Goodness knows when she would get Hetty King up a tree like this again. She meant to make the most of it.

"You should ask Miss Olivia there to give a few lessons," Peg went on. "Or your brother, Alec, for that matter. The only difference between you and me, Hetty, is that I say in public what you say behind closed doors."

Peter, who had heard plenty of what Hetty had to say behind closed doors, suddenly choked, sputtered and burst into open guffaws. Every gaze swung to him, as horrified as though he had suddenly been afflicted with lunacy. Worrying about his clothes and about his first visit to church, and then not having money for the collection plate, had left Peter so nervous that once he started laughing he couldn't help himself. Though he clapped his hand instantly over his mouth and pressed it so tight that his fingers went white, Peter was unable to stop. His gusts of laughter echoed from the solemn Presbyterian rafters, in spite of his most frantic efforts to stifle them.

"You're dead right, lad," Peg grinned. "Sure it would make a cat laugh."

With that, Peg gathered her shawl around her and swept towards the door, leaving the dignity of the congregation in ruins behind her. Reverend Brinsmead, seeing that his sheep had turned into a tiger and was stalking from the premises, made a belated, pleading gesture to stop her.

"Miss Bowen!"

His shout had no effect whatever on Peg, who was done with listening to missionaries and was marching rapidly out of sight.

Back inside the church, Peter's gaffaws had been smothered into a few wretched giggles. Felicity shrank down in mortification. Sara jabbed Peter fiercely with her toe.

"Stop it, Peter. You're only making things worse."

Reverend Leonard, who had been paralyzed by this unprecedented drama, suddenly came to life. This was his church, and it was up to him to restore order. Casting a reproachful look at Reverend Brinsmead, he began to hurry up the aisle.

"Quiet, quiet please. Mr. Boynton, would you kindly favor us with a medley on the organ?"

The organist, who had never seen such excitement in the little church, plunged into the opening hymn with all the vigor at his command. The two ministers got the service under way quickly. Reverend Leonard tried to divert everyone with a couple of thundering prayers, and Reverend Brinsmead told about polygamy among the natives, but the two never did regain the full attention of the congregation. Hetty sat rigid as a broomstick, while Felicity was too embarrassed by Peter to look up even once. Peter spent the rest of the service sunk in miserable dread, knowing that his employer was livid and Felicity would never speak to him again as long as he lived. Mrs. Sloane fairly strangled her hymnbook to death all through the sermon and the offering. When the final chord of the organ crashed, she rose to her feet and sailed out the door with Mrs. Tarbush at her side.

"Well, I never!" Mrs. Sloane spluttered as she stomped down the church steps. "In all my years—"

She couldn't think of anything in all her years shocking enough to compare with what had just happened to her

"The gall of that woman!" Mrs. Tarbush agreed.

Stephen Grant was dragging his family towards their buggy as fast as he could, perhaps to avoid any fresh questions about his house fire.

Behind him, Hetty marched out of the church with Peter Craig gripped in one hand and Sara in the other. Her face was sizzling with fury.

"That is the last straw, you two! You made a spectacle of yourselves, and of us, in front of the whole town of Avonlea. Sara Stanley, I ought to take you over my knee and give you a darn good spanking. And as for you, Peter Craig, you've exhausted the last of my generosity. As soon as I find a hired man to replace you, you're through. For good!"

It was Peter's greatest fear that he would lose his job at Rose Cottage, and now, it seemed, the worst had happened. When Hetty released both children with a shove and hustled off towards the buggy, Peter could only stand there, looking at Sara, utterly distraught. How would he live if he couldn't earn his way at Hetty King's?

Uncle Alec, trying to herd his own children out, overheard the scene and pushed his way through the departing throng, bent on rescue.

"Hetty, you're too hasty. Listen..." he called out to his sister. But it didn't do the least bit of good. Hetty wouldn't even look at him.

Peter was wringing his hands and struggling not to burst into tears in front of Felicity. If this was the result of trying Presbyterianism, Peter vowed never to go near any church in Avonlea again.

Chapter Five

That Sunday was one of those sparkling, sunny Prince Edward Island days on which it seemed illegal to do anything but enjoy oneself. Sara and her King cousins had been shell-hunting down on the beach, and now they were racing madly across the sloping, grassy pasture just outside Rose Cottage, waving their booty of seashells high above their heads. Edward Ray and his little sister, Clemmie, who was Cecily's best friend, raced with them, carefree and laughing. Clemmie and Cecily, being the smallest, struggled hard to keep up.

For Sara, though, the delight of such a perfect day was clouded by worry. How could she pretend everything was fine when Aunt Hetty wanted to fire Peter Craig?

Sara couldn't help feeling that Peter's predicament was partly her fault; after all, it was she who made him go to church that day. Why, oh why, did things have to turn out the way they did? Her only hope was with her Uncle Alec, who had taken Sara and Peter aside and promised that he'd try to change Hetty's mind, once she'd had a chance to calm down.

Peter Craig, meanwhile, was hard at work with Uncle Alec, fixing the fence that bordered the pasture. On a farm, fences could never be neglected or the animals might get out and ruin someone else's crop. Peter jockeyed the last, awkward rail into place while Alec, wielding a large pair of pliers, twisted the wire to hold it steady.

"Good work, Peter," Uncle Alec told him approvingly. "It won't be long before you're runnin' the farm on your own."

These were pretty grand words to say to a boy who had as good as been fired, and was only at Rose Cottage until someone else could be found. Uncle Alec admired the repairs for a moment, then hefted the black roll of fence wire to his shoulder. When he saw the anxious expression on Peter's face, he gave the boy's shoulder a pat.

"Well, I've got some chores to finish up, and I...I want to have a word with my sister."

Peter knew what the word would be about, and some of the worry left his young face. He had been trying to hide his apprehension ever since Hetty's harsh words after church. Now, with Alec King on his side, maybe, just maybe, everything was going to be put right.

Alec paused a moment, watching his own brood shouting merrily.

"There's no end to the trouble those kids get into," he said affectionately, then headed for Rose Cottage.

After Alec King had gone inside, Peter stood by the fence looking rather wistfully at the young people approaching. He was young too, and his toes fairly itched to be speeding along over the pasture grass. He could outrun Edward Ray any day, and longed to try. Better not even think about it, he decided. After the scene at the church, he was already in about as much trouble as he could manage at the moment.

As Peter sighed and headed for the woodpile, the children slowed their headlong gallop over the pasture hummocks. Edward grabbed the opportunity to catch up with Felicity. Tall for his age, handsome and strong, Edward had already set more than one or two hearts aflutter in the Avonlea public school.

"Why didn't you wait for me, Felicity?"

"Oh, Edward, I forgot."

Felicity hadn't forgotten at all. She just wanted to make Edward work hard for the privilege of her company. Edward reached eagerly into his pocket.

"I wanted to give you this shell."

He held out a beauty— pale cream, and speckled all over with blue. He had had to wade out into water over his knees to find it and retrieve it, just for Felicity. Felicity, who adored pretty things, added it to her basket. Edward grinned proudly from ear to ear, but soon found his rejoicing premature. Felicity handed him her basket to hold just so she could climb through the fence to talk to Peter Craig.

"Peter, why don't you come and play with us?" she asked sweetly.

Peter, who was surprised that Felicity even noticed his existence after her fury with him, sank his ax fiercely into a block of wood. When you were a hired boy practically tossed out on your ear, play was the last luxury you had time for. And Felicity knew this perfectly well.

"I can't. I have to finish my chores."

"Don't tell me you play with the hired boy," Edward shot over the fence, giving Peter his most disdainful sneer.

Felicity was delighted with the effect that merely speaking to Peter had on Edward. She turned around and gave Edward a wide-eyed look.

"Edward Ray, you're not jealous, are you?"

So! This was the secret of Felicity's sudden friendliness to Peter. Edward scowled all the harder, as if to say this was what happened when a fellow gave a girl a shell. Peter, to get away from whatever might be said next, flung down his ax and headed for Rose Cottage. As quickly as she could, Sara wriggled through the fence too and ran after him.

"Can't you play with us now, Peter? What's left to do?"

Sara's invitation was genuine, not just a false ploy as Felicity's had been. Peter stopped and looked back towards the other children.

"A lot. I've got to stack the wood, collect the eggs and..."

"It's not fair," Sara burst out. "You never have any time off." Since Sara lived at Rose Cottage, she knew how hard Peter really did work, his every day a constant struggle against the tasks that kept piling up ahead of him. She thought a moment, then brightened. "I know—we'll help you."

Edward Ray got huffy at once.

"Speak for yourself. I don't do farm work."

"Edward Ray, your grandfather was a farmer," Felicity pointed out. She seemed determined to torment Edward today and would use even Sara's innocent suggestions to do it.

"Well," Edward retorted ungraciously, "I don't intend to be one."

Oddly, it was Felix who actually put Sara's plan into action.

"Come on," he bubbled. "It'll be fun."

Only the satisfaction of putting Edward Ray in his place could have made Felix volunteer for hard work. He hopped through the fence towards the woodpile, and all the other children followed. All, that is, except Edward and Felicity.

"Clemmie, I'm gonna tell on you," Edward shouted vainly after his little sister, who was defecting with the others to Peter Craig's side.

Edward stayed firmly planted where he was. Before Felicity had a chance to decide which camp she was in, she was surprised by Olivia, returning in the buggy, which was now loaded with parcels of clothing she had collected for the mission.

"Aunt Olivia," Felicity exclaimed.

"Whoa," Olivia shouted to Blackie, who had been acting contrary all the way home. Blackie stopped by the fence and Olivia got gingerly down, making sure Blackie intended to stand still.

"Hello, Felicity. Be a dear and help me with my parcels. And Peter, can you put Blackie in the barn for me?"

Peter was almost invisible behind a huge armload of wood. Nevertheless, he heard Olivia's request.

"Yes, Miss Olivia," he sang out. He was always pleased to help Olivia.

"Thank you, Peter"

Olivia promptly loaded herself and Felicity with parcels and headed for the door of Rose Cottage.

Inside, Alec was having his promised talk with Hetty and stood by the stove, lighting his pipe. Alec always resorted to his pipe when he had some delicate persuading to do.

"Don't be hard on him, Hetty. You know, Peter's done a decent job fixing that fence. 'Course..." Alec took a long puff, "once the harvest is in, you will want to think about replacing it. And...the roof needs work."

"Oh Lord, what next?"

Hetty suspected her brother of making up work just so she would keep Peter around. Trust Alec to have a big soft spot for hired boys who took on far more than they could rightly do.

Just then, Olivia and Felicity came in, so heavily

laden they could scarcely see where they were going.

"I'm back," Olivia announced. "Oh, hello Alec. Put those right on the table, Felicity. Thank you, dear."

"You're welcome. Bye," returned Felicity, dropping the parcels and skipping right back out the door as fast as she could before one of them thought of something else for her to do. She had no intention of wasting such a nice day doing work.

"Goodbye," her father called as she disappeared.

"Well, what a day," sighed Olivia, removing her hat and smoothing her hair before the hall mirror. "Oh, guess who I saw in Markdale."

Alec raised his brows obligingly.

"Who?"

"Peter's mother. She looks so tired and worried, poor thing. There she is, struggling to make ends meet, reduced to being old Mrs. Connolly's housekeeper."

This sad plight failed to elicit any sympathy from Hetty, who now started watering her geraniums. Hetty was a strong believer in making one's own lot in life.

"Humph! In my opinion, Maude brought it on

herself. If she had had any sense, she never would have married Jack Craig."

"Well, she has put up with an awful lot, Hetty," put in Olivia, who was always ready to give people the benefit of the doubt—a habit that always irritated Hetty.

"If what I hear is true, he's in the right place now—behind bars."

"Yes, that should sober him up," Alec added placidly, taking another pull at his pipe. Jack Craig had been considered a headstrong young man who needed some reining in.

"I'm not sure Peter's in the right place, though, Alec," Hetty went on, determined to get back to their original topic before her brother got away. "He will never fill old Jake's shoes. Why, Jake would have had that fence rebuilt before I even knew it needed mending."

"No, you're right," Alec had to agree, "he will never replace old Jake. He knew this farm like the back of his hand, God rest his soul. But Peter, he's a good boy."

"Boy, yes. That, in a nutshell, is the problem," Hetty grumbled. "I have the farm to run, school to teach and Sara to take care of. I should never have let you talk me into hiring him in the first place."

Alec shifted himself away from the stove as though looking for a quick getaway. Hetty had a way of pointing out shortcomings, and Alec had no intention of letting her get started.

"Look, Hetty, I've told you. I'll look after anything that he can't handle, so stop fretting."

And, with that, Alec followed his daughter's example and escaped to the outdoors, where the sunshine was sparkling and none of the tasks still waiting to be done were going to argue back.

Chapter Six

Outside Rose Cottage, Felix had actually kept his promise about helping Peter with his chores. He and Peter were just tossing the last of the wood onto the woodpile.

"There," breathed Peter, "all done. Thanks, Felix."

Felix stepped back, pleased with himself for helping, and strolled over to where the other children were sitting. Peter followed him but stopped by the fence, not quite sure he should join the group.

"Come on, let's go play," Felix cried, anxious to enjoy the benefits of his labor.

Sara jumped up.

Now that Peter could join them in their fun, her spirits brightened considerably. She could think of many delightful things to do with such a lovely afternoon

"I know—let's play blindman's buff by the pond."

Edward Ray almost jumped up too, but stopped himself when he spotted Peter hovering in the background.

"I hate that game," Edward scoffed in that superior manner he could affect so annoyingly when he wished. He would have just stretched out on the grass again if it hadn't been for Felix. Felix didn't hate any game, and he was already off and running towards the pond.

"Last one there's a dirty rotten egg," Felix shouted over his shoulder, taking great leaps among the daisies.

Sara ran over to Peter, who was at that moment untying Blackie from the fence. Putting Blackie in the barn was yet one more task he had promised to do.

"Come on, Peter. You can put the horse in the barn after, when we help you gather the eggs."

Peter looked rather guiltily at Blackie. Eggs might wait quietly, but not horses. Blackie had

had a long, strenuous trot to Markdale and back, and now she was switching her tail the way she did when she was very displeased. Besides being quite thirsty, Blackie wanted to get her hot harness off and munch on the oats she knew very well were waiting in the barn.

"Well..."

"Come on," Sara begged, and she, too, started to run. "It'll be fun."

Peter, who already had Blackie untied, watched longingly as Felix, Cecily and Clemmie vanished over the hill, followed by Sara and Felicity. He hesitated, knowing he really ought to take care of the horse first. Then, tempted by the joys of a childhood game, Peter tied Blackie to the fence again and set off towards the pond. Edward Ray, smiling maliciously, quietly undid the loop in Blackie's reins before he, too, followed after the rest.

The pond was an intriguing place. For there were clumps of goldenrod higher than Cecily's head, stands of reeds on the shore, bullfrogs and sometimes even ducks on the mirror-smooth patch of water. Once there, everyone except Edward flung themselves into blindman's buff. There was lots of giggling, teasing and high spirits. Felicity, who was "it," tried to catch the others who circled around her, holding hands. Edward Ray deliberately hung to one side as though fancying himself too dignified for such silly goings-on. The truth was that Edward wasn't a good sport about any game that didn't show him off to advantage. No way did he want to join a circle in which Felicity, blindfolded, had an equal chance of catching him or Peter Craig.

Peter played blindman's buff with all his might. Games were so scarce in his hard-working young life that he had no idea when he might ever get to have this much fun again. He dodged in and out, his hair flying in the breeze, his round face flushed and merry. For the briefest while, he forgot all about his endless chores and all about Blackie.

"Hey, catch me," he dared Felicity. "Over here."

To make sure Felicity wouldn't miss, Peter leaned towards her—and fell straight into her outstretched hands. Felicity clutched him instantly and guessed his name before she tore the blindfold from her face.

"I knew it was you, Peter," Felicity told him, as though seeing through blindfolds were one of her special powers.

Felicity took care to ignore Edward, knowing how it irritated him. Indeed, she let go of Peter and with a giggle started to run, her chestnut hair flying behind her, towards the quivering stand of birches to one side of Rose Cottage. Accepting the challenge, Peter lit out after her, leaving the others behind. He caught up with Felicity right in the middle of the trees and grasped her by the arm.

"I've got you," he grinned. And then, because he was squeezing her arm too tightly, he switched to gripping her hand.

Even Felicity could forget her dignity sometimes. All pink and breathless from the run, she found herself grinning back. Only when she heard the others galloping up did she come to herself, her surprise swiftly giving way to indignation.

"How dare you!" she squawked, jerking her hand away.

Peter stared at her in astonished consternation as the other children surrounded them.

"What's going on?" Edward demanded, as though anything concerning Felicity was his personal business.

"He tried to hold my hand!"

From Felicity's tone, you'd have thought

Felix also had apparently been searching his conscience
and not liking what he found there.
"We were so mean to him,
and he never did anything to us."

"Can't you do the simplest thing? The horse could break a leg."

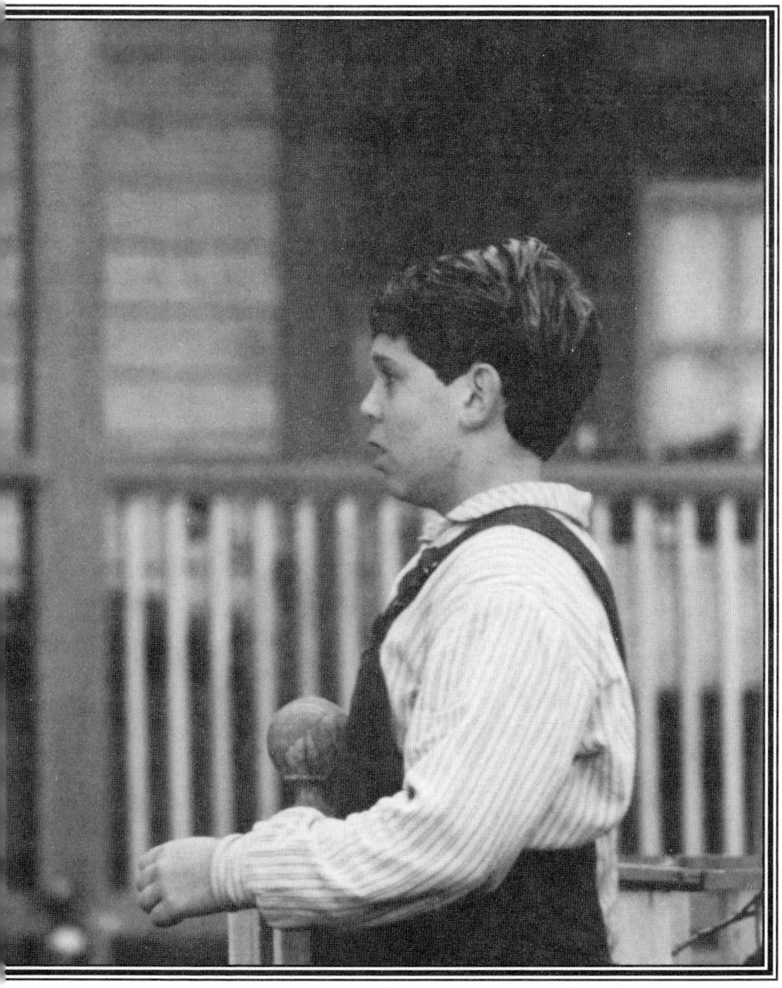

Peter hung his head. "I'm sorry."

Hetty's cheeks were quivering with fury. "I've had enough. You're going back to where you belong. Go on, now—inside, pack your bag."

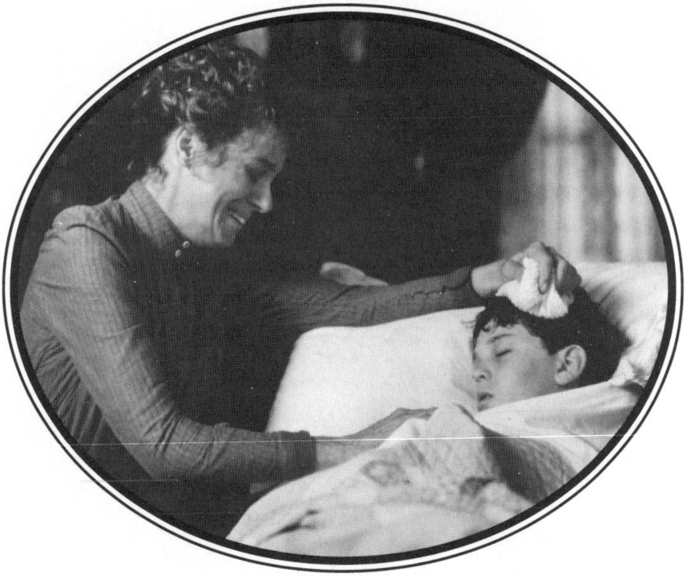

"Mama?" Peter's voice was a mere thread, incredulous and raspy.

Mrs. Craig sank down on the bed, immediately picking up Peter's hand. She was trying very hard to keep her own from shaking.

"Peter? Peter, I'm here. You're going to be all right."

Peter had also tried to steal all ten of her fingers and put them in his pocket.

"He tried what?"

Edward had had enough of taking a back seat to a hired boy, and Felicity's complaint was all the excuse he needed. He marched straight over to Peter and, without so much as a by-your-leave, pushed Peter backwards into the fence. The fence might have withstood inquisitive jersey cows and leaning horses, but not young boys about to get into a fight. It registered its disapproval by collapsing instantly—breaking right in the spot Peter had helped Alec fix not an hour before.

Peter and the fence crashed down into a tumble of splintered rails and flailing legs. The noise was too much for Blackie. With a roll of her eyes, she took a jump sideways and then bolted, buggy and all, straight down the road.

"Peter," Felicity shrieked, putting both hands to her mouth in horror.

Peter now had far worse problems than girls who accused him of trying to hold their hands.

"The horse," he croaked, disentangling himself from the fence just in time to see the buggy madly careening on two wheels behind the galloping Blackie. For a hired boy already fired once, this was disaster in the making. As fast as his legs could carry him, Peter charged after the wayward animal, with the rest of the children in hot pursuit.

Chapter Seven

Unfortunately, runaway buggies are noisy things, and inside Rose Cottage, Alec, Hetty and Olivia were immediately alarmed.

"What is it now?" Hetty demanded.

Alec, closest to the window, sprang up out of his chair.

"The bloody horse has run off!"

All of the grown-ups ran out the door just in time to see the children dashing onto the road and Peter shouting, "Blackie, wait!" at the top of his lungs.

"What in Heaven's name is going on?" cried Hetty, as though the situation weren't perfectly clear, even to an idiot.

Uncle Alec headed out onto the road himself after the horse. His head was full of the terrible trouble a horse and buggy on their own could get into.

"Don't worry. I'll get her back."

Olivia, too, picked up her skirts and started to run after them. Aunt Hetty was more interested in the culprit responsible for the calamity, and she picked him out immediately.

"Peter Craig, you come back here at once!"

Hetty's whipping command stopped Peter right in the middle of a step, even though he was well down the road after the buggy. Positively quaking in his boots, he turned back.

"Yes, ma'am," he panted out in a very small, very miserable voice. He knew he was finished now for sure.

"Who left that horse untied?"

"I guess I'm to blame, ma'am," Peter admitted.

Even in the midst of disaster, it never occurred to Peter to try to pin the blame on anyone else, as a less honest boy might have done. Yet honesty didn't make up for the accident or prevent Hetty from raking over Peter's failings.

"Can't you do the simplest thing? The horse could break a leg."

Peter hung his head even lower. He wished the ground would open right then and there and swallow him up.

"I'm sorry."

Hetty probably wished the ground would swallow him too. Since it refused to oblige, she saw she would have to deal with Peter herself. When Hetty truly got worked up over a thing, she often spoke before she could think. Her cheeks were quivering with fury as she waved one arm towards the house.

"I've had enough. You're going back where you belong. Go on, now—inside, pack your bag. Go on."

As though there weren't already enough people streaming down the road to catch ten horses, Hetty, too, set out after Blackie, leaving poor Peter standing alone in horrified dismay. As he slowly made his way up the steps of Rose Cottage, the other children and Olivia came running back just in time to meet Hetty.

"Uncle Alec caught the mare," Sara announced, panting for breath and infinitely relieved that neither horse nor buggy had come to harm, "'cause she stopped for a drink down by the stream. Where's Peter?"

Peter's whereabouts no longer concerned Hetty. She turned a severe eye on Sara herself. She had worked up a good head of steam over Peter and needed one more child to expend it upon.

"I can't tell you the times I've told you to leave that boy alone, Sara Stanley."

With that, Hetty turned and marched towards the house.

Felicity's nose went up in a fair imitation of her aunt as she hastily put herself on the side of power.

"We've been far too nice to him all along. Fancy, a hired boy trying to hold my hand!"

Felicity did, however, look secretly pleased that her hand was in demand somewhere. Edward didn't miss this and rushed in to reinforce the attack. Both Edward and Felicity were guilty of starting the ruckus that had frightened Blackie in the first place, so naturally they tried to bury this little detail as quickly as possible.

"What do you expect from a boy whose father's in prison?"

"Maybe he's innocent, just like my father," Sara flung back. "He never did the things that they accused him of."

"Maybe, Felicity said "but you could be safe doubting it."

Tossing off this airy comment was a big mistake on Felicity's part. In an instant, Sara was bristling from head to toe like a roused-up cat. Sara thought her father the most wonderful man in the world, and woe betide anyone who dared hint otherwise.

"You bite your tongue, Felicity King! My father never did anything wrong!"

"I was talking about Peter's father," Felicity amended hastily, more than a little taken aback at the reaction she had provoked.

Turning her back on Felicity, Sara stormed into the house. Felicity stood still a moment, then started after her.

Upset, Sara dashed upstairs where she ran smack into Peter, standing in the hall with his bag slung over his shoulder. He looked glum enough to bring on sleet and rain.

"Peter, what are you doing?" Sara cried, openly alarmed at the signs of imminent departure.

"Your Aunt Hetty let me go. She told me to go pack my bag."

"What?"

Peter hung his head wretchedly, for it was beginning to sink into him what getting fired really meant.

"My Ma was counting on me. I let her down when she needed me the most."

"Oh no!"

Sara turned and dashed straight back down to the kitchen, where she found her kind-hearted Aunt Olivia already started on the same argument Sara had in mind.

"Hetty, please, give him one more chance," Olivia pleaded.

But Hetty was still steaming and in no mood to listen to soft words. Once she had made up her mind, she would not be deflected from her path.

"Olivia, you're all heart and no brains. I feel like I'm trying to run a farm with three children—Sara, Peter and you."

Sara spoke up, bursting with urgency.

"Aunt Hetty, you mustn't let Peter go. It's not his fault. I saw him tie up the horse. I really did."

With support from a new quarter, Olivia pressed Peter's case.

"You know how much this job means to him, Hetty."

"Aunt Hetty, if you let Peter stay, I promise I'll leave him alone. I won't even speak to him," Sara vowed, with all the heartfelt urgency she was capable of. She remembered, very uneasily, how she had tempted Peter away from his work to play. If only Peter could stay, Sara was willing to seal her lips with packing tape and glue.

Aching sincerity and ringing promises didn't cut much ice with Hetty. Sara had been using fine words and voicing grand sentiments since the first day she had arrived at Rose Cottage, but Hetty would not be swayed.

"How many times have I heard that before, Sara? Hmm?"

"I cross my heart," Sara added earnestly, matching her words with a dramatic gesture. "And anyway, if you let him go, where will he stay? He can't stay with his mother. They don't have a home any more."

This point was a very powerful one and, at last, put even Hetty on the defensive. Her mouth closed tighter and she paced the kitchen distractedly.

"I wanted to help Peter and his mother. I really did, Sara. It just isn't working. I need a proper hired hand like old Jake. Besides, Peter will be better off somewhere else. Perhaps his mother could—"

"But you promised to keep him here so that he could go to school," Olivia interjected, seeing the crack in Hetty's armor. It was very important to Hetty that children go to school.

Sara rushed in quickly to help.

"That's right, Aunt Hetty. You can't break your promise."

In the King family, the word of honor was sacred. Sara had Hetty on that score, just as she'd had her in the matter of wearing plain clothes to church.

At this moment, Peter trudged in carrying his pitifully light bag of belongings.

"I'm ready to go, ma'am," he mumbled, his face long and downcast.

Hetty really did have a good heart, if one ever managed to find it amidst all her prickles. One look at Peter's woebegone figure apparently gave her second thoughts. She let out a sighing breath.

"Well, Peter, perhaps I was a bit hasty."

Peter's gaze swiftly rose from the floor.

"Ma'am?" he whispered in surprise and tremulous hope.

"It's true. Those children had no business bothering you. But then, you should never have left that horse untied. Someone could have been seriously hurt. But as long as you learn from your mistakes and try harder to finish your duties so you can go to school, well, then...yes, you can stay on."

The fortress had collapsed, and Sara could barely keep from dancing around the kitchen. A dance of victory wouldn't have been very politic, though, so Sara satisfied herself with simple gratitude.

"Thank you, Aunt Hetty."

"But you're probationary, mind you," Hetty warned, all bristly again lest anyone think she was too soft a touch. "Everything depends on how well you do."

Peter felt ready to accept twenty years of probation if it meant he could keep his job.

"You won't be sorry, ma'am," he declared gratefully. Then he ran smiling from the kitchen before anything could happen to this miraculous reprieve.

Grinning all over, Sara followed after him. Already she looked as though she were going to have a very hard time keeping her resolution to leave Peter alone and not drop more temptations in his way.

Chapter Eight

Early the next morning, Sara and Peter walked along the road in company with Sara's King cousins. They wore their sturdy school clothes and carried their lunches in brown paper bags. Felix, though he had just come from a hearty breakfast, was already helping himself to a sandwich.

"Felix, you're supposed to wait until lunchtime," Felicity scolded, regarding herself as a guardian of food in the King household.

"I'm starving," Felix protested, taking another enormous bite. He was eleven, just the age when boys need food put into them with shovels.

"You're always starving."

Felicity didn't think much of hungry boys, especially when she had to do a lot of the work of feeding them.

Peter, striding beside her, wasn't thinking of food, or even, amazingly, of Felicity. Today was a very big day for Peter. Hetty was making good on her promise that he should go to school.

Peter was lucky that Hetty had a conscience in the matter. A good many other employers tried to squeeze as much work as they could out of hired boys, and considered themselves terribly cheated should anyone even mention time off for education. Peter had a happy, fearful, faraway look in his eyes, as if new horizons were opening before him and he was just working up the nerve to approach them.

"I'm gonna do my best. I'm gonna prove to Miss King that I can do it," Peter vowed. Peter hoped fervently that reading, writing and arithmetic would make up for the runaway buggy. He had been reprieved twice now, and was terribly eager to make good in Hetty's eyes. "But," he now came to the sticky part, "I don't know about school. I've never spent much time at it before."

Sara gave him a reassuring smile. She had a

personal interest in Peter's success and lots of useful experience to share. Before coming to Avonlea, she had had tutors. But, in spite of all the money her father had paid them, they had given her such a spotty education that everyone in the Avonlea school had been appalled at her ignorance.

"Don't worry, Peter. I missed a lot of school too. But now I'm nearly all caught up."

Doubt and brave hope struggled in Peter's face. He not only wanted to impress Hetty. It was also the wish of his dear mother's heart that he somehow get his schooling, even if he did have to work as a hired boy.

He didn't get a chance to say any more because Edward and Clemmie Ray were waiting for them where the road forked off to the Ray place. The very first thing Edward did was look Peter up and down and fling him an openly derisive snicker.

"Well, look who's here—the prince of the barnyard."

Edward hated the idea of Peter being underfoot at school, where Felicity might talk to him again.

"Shut your mouth, Edward Ray," Sara spat fiercely, leaping to Peter's defense. Sara thought she knew how Blackie had got loose, and she felt that Edward was a positive danger to Peter. She meant to prevent any more trouble if it were the last thing she did.

"Sara!" Felicity scolded. "Pay no attention to her, Edward."

Well! Felicity was back on Edward's side. Triumphantly, Edward fell in beside Felicity, quite squeezing Peter out. While Peter's face fell, Felicity and Edward walked a little ahead, pointedly distancing themselves. Felix kept right on eating while Sara scowled at Felicity's rudeness. Cecily, who had been too busy whispering to Clemmie to bother about the older children, suddenly peered into the distance.

"Uh-oh, there's Peg Bowen," Cecily warned, pointing across the field to where Peg could be seen, like a wavering ghost in the morning mist rising from the grass. Peg carried an old wicker basket today and bent down now and then. She was often seen out in the country like this. How else was she to gather the plants she needed for her magic spells?

Edward forgot all about looking pleased with himself and spun around.

"Run, before she sees us. She'll put a spell on us," he sputtered. The next minute, Edward was hightailing it as fast as he could down the road.

At this show of courage, the rest of the children started to run too—all except Peter, who defiantly kept walking at his own leisurely pace. He wasn't going to run away from Peg Bowen picking herbs in a pasture.

Up ahead, Sara slowed her pace to a walk. They were almost at the schoolyard now.

"She's not even looking at us," she said, feeling foolish at their hasty flight.

"She doesn't need to look at us," Clemmie returned, panting mightily as she struggled to keep up with the rest of the group. "My ma says she's got eyes in the back of her head," she added breathlessly.

"That's impossible!" Next thing, Sara thought, Mrs. Ray would be claiming that Peg could sprout wings and fly around at night like a bat.

Once Sara slowed, all the other children did so too. Nervously, they looked back to see Peg Bowen approach the fence near Peter and eye him closely, as if about to say something, when Edward's shout cut the air.

"Look. Peter is Peg Bowen's friend. Peter Craig is a witch's helper!" Edward, nonplussed to see that Peter didn't seem at all afraid of Peg, didn't want to give any of the children—Felicity in particular—any chance to comment on his own precipitous flight.

The other children laughed at Edward's taunt, and he felt a little better. Saying nothing, Peg Bowen continued on her way.

At school, all the children took their seats, except Peter. Since the school was for children of all ages, Hetty couldn't be sure where to seat him until she had discovered just how far his education had progressed. Until then, he would have to stand behind her at the front of the class.

Hetty went to the blackboard and chalked up a problem in addition.

"Now," she said to Peter, "let's see what you can do. Can you add that?"

Like a prisoner at the gallows, Peter stood at the board with the chalk in his hand. He stared at the white numbers glaring back at him. He chewed on one corner of his lip, shifted from one foot to the other and frowned as hard as he could, but no answer appeared in his head.

"Um...three, plus one is, um...um...Don't know, ma'am," he finally had to confess.

"Even I can do that," Felix whispered to the boy behind him.

Hetty pursed her lips. Peter was a very large

boy not to be able to add three and one.

"Well then, let's see about your spelling. 'The stalwart soldier stormed the castle wall.' Write it."

Peter was being introduced with a vengeance to the perils of education. If arithmetic was daunting, writing and spelling were almost enough to do a fellow in. Gamely, Peter gripped the chalk harder and managed a large "S" on the blackboard. Unfortunately, "S" was the only letter he produced. The rest of the word attached to the "S" immediately shrouded itself in impenetrable mystery.

"St...st...stal...stal...," Hetty prompted. She tapped her pointer against the palm of her hand as she waited, then dropped it on her desk.

"That's enough Peter. That's enough."

Felicity leaned over to Edward Ray. "He can't even write," she chortled incredulously.

Edward, who could write very well, began to look very puffed up indeed. He knew how Felicity admired education.

"He's dumb as a post," Edward murmured back, under his breath.

Sara overheard him clearly. Her eyes narrowed at once.

"William the Conquerer couldn't write, either."

She shut her mouth just as Hetty shot a look in her direction. Talking out of turn was a grave offense in the Avonlea school, and those who indulged in it took great care not to get caught.

Peter, anxious to redeem himself from his two ignominious failures, picked up William's name.

"I know about history, ma'am."

Hetty looked both hopeful and highly skeptical at the same time.

"Well, really? Can you name the kings of England?"

If she had expected to unsettle Peter with this huge assignment, she failed.

"Starting with William the Conquerer or the Tudors?" Peter asked matter-of-factly.

"The Tudors will do."

"Henry VII, Henry VIII, Edward VI, Mary Tudor, Elizabeth, James I, Charles I, Charles II, James II," Peter rolled out all in one breath.

Hetty was completely taken aback, as was the rest of the class, including Edward Ray. Peter Craig did not appear to be quite as dumb as Edward had expected.

"Very impressive, Peter Craig," Hetty praised.

With this encouragement, Peter decided to show that he not only knew the Tudor rulers, he knew the details of their individual lives as well.

"Edward VI was only ten when he came to the throne, ma'am."

Peter couldn't prevent himself from sliding a glance at Felicity to see how she was taking his success. Felicity was sitting quite upright with surprise, and Edward Ray was glowering again.

"And where did you learn all this?" Hetty inquired. She couldn't imagine how a hired boy knew such things.

"My Ma used to read to me from the history book."

This was rather a different picture of life in the family of a jailbird than was generally accepted. Hetty King perked up considerably, for she was always on the watch for promising pupils. She looked Peter up and down as though she had never actually seen him before.

"Hmm, well...with a memory like that, there's hope for you yet. Mind you..." Hetty couldn't let Peter think anything was going to be easy just because he had a good memory. "...It will require a great deal of effort to catch up properly. Now, where shall I put you? Oh...um...ah!" Hetty hit upon an idea. "Edward Ray is our best student. You can sit next to him."

Avonlea scholars sat in twos at double desks, so it was very important to get a deskmate one liked. Hetty had no idea of the antipathy Edward had for Peter, and wouldn't have paid attention to it if she had.

Edward's face froze in disbelief as Peter walked down the aisle and slid into the seat next to his. Felicity glared as though, just by sitting there, Peter were committing some grave affront.

Peter was far from happy with the arrangement himself, but he was so pleased to be going to school that he would have sat uncomplainingly with one of Reverend Brinsmead's cannibals. Just as Edward was getting ready to sneer again, he broke out into a whole series of sneezes instead, which rather put paid to his self-important affectations.

"Coughs and sneezes spread diseases," Hetty said automatically. "So you'd best watch out for that cold, Edward. Besides, I'll be needing you to assist Peter with his studies over the next several weeks."

This announcement choked out Edward's next burst of coughs. He and Peter stared at each other with unfeigned astonishment. Barely hiding his misgivings, Peter turned to Sara. Sara could only shrug and lower her eyes.

Chapter Nine

Edward Ray should have paid heed to Hetty's advice. Before scarcely any time had passed, he was a very sick boy, barely able to totter about his own house. In the Ray kitchen, his mother had him bending over a basin with a towel over his head. Into the basin she poured boiling water from the kettle, so that he could inhale the vapor. Mrs. Ray was a large, bony woman who feared nothing on this Presbyterian earth except illness. The least little sniffle in her family threw her into utter consternation.

"Oh, Edward, I pray this is just a cold and not the influenza. The influenza has never gone very well with the Rays."

News about his hereditary weaknesses did little to perk up the patient's spirits. The kitchen fell oddly silent. As Edward inhaled a great lungful of steam, Mrs. Ray put the kettle back on the stove to heat more water. And Edward's sister, Clemmie, sadly wondered what she would do if her big brother didn't get better soon. It was true that he could be mean, and he did bully her sometimes, but she didn't want anything so bad as the influenza to happen to him.

Suddenly, the Rays' dog, who slept behind the stove when he could, set up such a clamor that Clemmie ran to the window to see what was causing it.

"Who is it, Clemmie?" Mrs. Ray demanded, annoyed. She was trying to balance the hot kettle with one hand and keep Edward's head over the steam with the other.

Clemmie's eyes went round as silver dollars. "It's the witch of Avonlea!"

Peg Bowen barely got up to the porch before the door flew open and Mrs. Ray appeared in the doorway, blocking it as effectively as would a wall. She was also doing her best to restrain the dog. Mrs. Ray believed in scary watchdogs. The one she was holding by the collar was a brindled monster who looked as though he ate up foolish intruders for mid-morning snacks. He was doing his best now to earn his keep by snarling and barking at the top of his lungs.

"Shush, shush," Mrs. Ray hissed uselessly at the dog. "Peg Bowen, what are you doing here?"

Mrs. Ray had strands of damp hair flying loose, and her face was flushed red from filling Edward's basin with boiling water. All this, on top of a ferocious scowl, made her uninviting indeed. But Peg spoke up, undaunted. "I heard your boy's in a bad way. I've got a remedy here. It should keep the fever down."

Peg had brought with her some well-chosen herbs tied up in a cloth bag, which she now held out before her. But Mrs. Ray reacted as though Peg were offering her a handful of poisonous snakes. In all of Avonlea, Mrs. Ray was one of the most heatedly outspoken against Peg's freewheeling style of life.

"I don't want your remedy, or your witchcraft. You leave this property immediately, you hear, or I'll set the dog on you!"

The dog, as though it understood English, set up an even greater racket and struggled wildly to get free of Mrs. Ray's grasp.

Peg regarded its bared fangs fearlessly. "You can always size a person up by the kind of dog she keeps."

With an outraged snort, Mrs. Ray dragged the dog back into the kitchen again and slammed the door right in Peg's face. Peg stood glowering at the knocker for a moment, for she had glimpsed Edward inside slumped weakly over the steaming basin. Even though the Ray house was now as closed against her as if it had a moat and drawbridge, Peg knew something had to be done. Shaking her head, she turned and hiked away.

• • •

When Peg was set on something, it took a lot more than a snarling dog and a slammed door to put her off. She calculated her friends in Avonlea and then headed straight over to Rose Cottage. There she found Peter Craig, brushing down Blackie out beside the barn. It was Peter whom Peg had come to see.

"That Mrs. Ray is a mean-spirited old harpy," Peg grated out without preamble as she crunched across the gravel. "What I wouldn't give to tell that woman what I really think of her—her and all the Sunday Christians in this town! You aren't afraid of me, are you, lad?"

Peter had been tugging at a knot in Blackie's mane. He wanted to please Hetty by making the mare shine like a piece of new coal. He shook his head sturdily.

"No."

And he kept on with his work to prove it. Ever since the fiasco in church, Peter had felt more than a sneaking sympathy for anyone who was the target of Avonlea's rudeness.

Peg pushed her hat back with satisfaction.

"Didn't think so. I've been watching you. You're just like your father, Jack Craig."

If Peg wanted Peter's full attention, she certainly had it now. Peter let go of Blackie's mane and turned to Peg. He wouldn't have run away now if Peg had started firing cannons.

"Really, I am?"

Like any boy separated from his parents, Peter longed desperately to hear anything he could about his father.

"Good man." Peg nodded. "Don't let anyone tell you otherwise. He was never afraid to speak his mind, which ain't easy in a town like this. Folks call you crazy if you don't think exactly like they think. Now," Peg got straight to the reason for her visit, "I want you to do something for me. I want you to take this package to Edward Ray's mother. I've no use for her, but the boy's deathly ill, and this will bring his fever down."

"Deathly ill?" Peter exclaimed, first surprised and then alarmed.

Peg bobbed her head again.

"You've got a horse, and the boy's in a bad way. So will you take it?"

"Well, I don't know," Peter mumbled, confused by the request and not at all sure how much liberty he was allowed to take with Blackie. Then, seeing the urgency on Peg's weathered face, and thinking of Edward gravely sick, he decided to take the risk. There were just some things even a hired boy didn't feel free to refuse.

"I'll take it."

"Knew you would."

Peg handed Peter the herbs, and Peter hoisted himself up on Blackie's back. Blackie gave a snort of surprise, for she had been almost asleep, enjoying her grooming.

"Now you tell her to put it in water, boil it up and make him drink it."

Peter committed these instructions to memory and started Blackie off towards the gate.

"And mind you," Peg called after him, "don't tell her who gave it to you or she won't take it from you, neither."

Peter knew this well enough. He kicked Blackie into a clumsy canter towards the Ray house. When he arrived and slid down from his mount, he knocked on the door. After a long moment, Mrs. Ray, looking more frazzled than ever, opened the door.

"Yes?"

"I'm Peter Craig, the hired boy over at Rose Cottage," Peter told her by way of hasty introduction. He didn't want Mrs. Ray to think just anybody would gallop up and knock on her door. Mrs. Ray at once became more polite.

"Oh, yes—Peter. What can I do for you?"

"We heard Edward has a bad fever. I've got something that might make him better."

Peter held out the bag of herbs which, luckily, Mrs. Ray didn't recognize. She took it from Peter's hand, not even able to tell it smacked of witchcraft.

"Well, that's very kind of you, Peter."

Peter then remembered to relay Peg's instructions.

"You're to put it in water, boil it up and give him some. Every half hour," he added, hoping it would sound more professional.

Mrs. Ray absorbed the information carefully.

"Oh, well, tell Hetty I'm much obliged."

Peter had no intention of telling Hetty any such thing. After Mrs. Ray went back inside, clutching the remedy, he got back on Blackie and hightailed it for Rose Cottage before any troublesome questions could come his way.

But if Peter thought he could escape questions, he was mistaken. At least one inhabitant of Rose Cottge missed very little and was curious about everything. Sara followed Peter to the barn and watched while he filled up a bucket at the bin full of chicken feed.

"Peter? Peter, what were you doing with Peg Bowen?"

Head down, Peter started towards the chicken pen.

"Nothin'."

"What were you talking to her about? Aunt Hetty's all upset."

So, Hetty had seen Peg too. Peter groaned inwardly, not sure whether his probation stretched to cover commerce with witches. There seemed no end of observant eyes around Rose Cottage. And, as if to prove it, Hetty herself stepped through the barn door.

"Peter Craig, I don't want you talking to that Bowen woman any more, do you understand? It will just encourage her to come round."

"But she asked me to deliver something," Peter protested, just as Felix and Felicity appeared behind their aunt. Inside of a very few minutes, quite a crowd was gathering to inquire into his affairs.

"Nor do I want you running errands for her. She's an out-and-out lunatic. Is that clear?"

"Yes, Miss Hetty," Peter answered, ready to say just about anything to get himself off the hook.

After Hetty left, Felix stuck his hands in his

pockets and screwed up his face at Peter.

"Edward's right. Peg Bowen's teaching you witchcraft."

Before Peter could reply, Felix ran off, leaving only Felicity behind. Felicity accorded Peter such a brief, dismissive glance that Peter despaired of ever being her friend.

"Sara, I thought you promised Aunt Hetty that you wouldn't speak to Peter any more. Are you coming?"

Felicity stepped towards the door, fully expecting Sara to follow. But Felicity, having caught Sara once again breaking the rules, was looking far too self-satisfied. Sara wouldn't pay her the least attention. Instead, she turned to Peter again, and Felicity had no choice but to leave all by herself.

Chapter Ten

The King orchard was the pride of the King family, and one of the finest orchards on Prince Edward Island. It had been started by the very first King to settle around Avonlea, and had been added to ever since. Whenever anything really significant happened in the King family, it was still the custom to honor the event by planting a new green sapling. Consequently, every spreading tree had a story of its own. A walk through the orchard was like a stroll straight through the history of the Kings, and of Avonlea.

Historical or not, though, all the trees produced loads of apples, and the apples had to be picked. Today, Peter was put to work with Alec in the orchard, heaving bushel after heavy bushel onto the wagon behind the team. More bushels, in a seemingly endless row, sat waiting at the feet of dozens more trees.

This was very hard work for such a young boy, and the necessary effort made Peter turn quite white around the corners of his mouth. But he kept working doggedly. A hired boy could not plop down on the grass and munch apples at his leisure as the King children, along with Sara and Clemmie, were at that moment doing. Though they all carried baskets on their arms, they had long ago stopped apple-picking. Instead, they were lounging in the dappled shade while Peter did the sweating. Felix, forever hungry, took a huge bite out of a russet. Felicity wrinkled her nose with distaste.

"Ugh! There's a worm in that apple, and you just swallowed it, you little piggy."

If he were going to be called a piggy, he might as well act like one. Felix immediately spat out the mouthful of apple he had been chewing on. Like a good many younger brothers, he loved to disgust his sister.

"If there's a worm in here, you find it, Felicity."

He rolled his eyes comically and pitched the rest of the apple at his sister. Very annoyed, she barely managed to bat away the much-eaten core.

"You have the best orchard and the biggest farm," Clemmie said to Cecily. "My Ma says you're rich, richer than anyone else in Avonlea."

Felicity overheard this. Instantly, she took umbrage. Imagine the Rays discussing her family's financial status! Whatever Mrs. Ray had said, it was certain to have been uncomplimentary.

"My father works very, very hard," Felicity asserted firmly, just to make sure Clemmie and the rest of the Rays knew that none of the King possessions were the result of idle gain.

"Still, it's not fair."

Clemmie was too young to understand how an orchard is planted, nourished and tended over generations. She saw only whispering green vistas with branches just right for climbing and laden with more juicy apples than one girl could eat in five lifetimes. Clemmie loved apples, and the Rays had no orchard at all.

"Of course it's fair," Felicity shot back, leaping yet more vigorously to the defense of her family. "Grandpa King was one of the first settlers on the Island, and since we were here first, it's only fair that our family is the most prosperous. Grandpa King planted a tree for each of us the day we were born so we would each have our own."

Now Clemmie was truly impressed. Her eyes went shiny at the idea of having one of the sweet-smelling, heavily laden trees especially for one's own.

"You're so lucky you were born in the King family."

Felicity flicked a leaf from her skirt as if to say that being born a King was only her due, and that those who hadn't been born Kings simply weren't deserving of the honor. She peered over her shoulder at Peter, who was struggling past, lugging yet another brimming bushel basket.

"Well, I'm certainly glad that I wasn't born poor," she said, just loud enough for Peter to hear. "That would be awful."

Peter's cheeks suddenly burned hot and red. He turned his head away quickly so that Felicity wouldn't see and heaved the bushel up onto the wagon.

Sara noticed Peter's discomfort and swiftly got down from the branch on which she had been sitting. If she couldn't exactly take Felicity to task in front of Peter, she could try to distract her. As a hint that they should all get back to work, Sara climbed halfway up the ladder leaning into the branches above Felicity's head. Felicity didn't get up, but she tidied the fruit in the basket beside her.

"What are you going to do with your apples, Sara?" she asked. Another benefit of being a King was that the children got to keep some of the apples they picked that day.

Sara shrugged. "I haven't decided yet."

"I'm going to sell my apples and give the money to the missionary fund on Sunday," Cecily piped up. Cecily had been enormously impressed by the Reverend Brinsmead's thrilling tales and felt her contribution would be well spent should it keep one more missionary from the stew pot.

"I'm going to sell mine and use the money to buy a new hat to wear," Felicity announced. She was much less concerned with the fate of missionaries than with how she looked when they were talking to her in church.

It was no accident that Peter had parked the team and wagon so close by. As he worked, Peter listened hungrily to all the easy talk. Finally, in spite of Felicity's jibe, he could contain himself no longer.

"I sure wish I had a tree of my own," he said out loud, and far more wistfully than he had intended. Though he couldn't have put it into words, what Peter's heart longed for were all the things a tree meant in this orchard—security, a prosperous farm, a close-knit family, a place of his own. Peter's folks had wandered from place to place, almost as the wind took them. They never owned land and were buried where they died, left to be forgotten when the family moved on.

Felicity understood none of this. She only saw a disheveled hired boy aspiring to what only true Kings were entitled to.

"You do?" she answered with a curl of her lip. "Well, there is one orchard tree you can have. It's over there...the dwarf tree." She pointed to a squat, lopsided tree festooned with gnarled, green-looking fruit. "The apples are so sour, the pigs won't even eat them. But I'm sure they're good enough for you."

Felicity's first few words had brought a piercing gleam of hope into Peter's face, but one glance at the deformed tree informed him that Felicity was only making fun of him again. He quivered, exactly as though a pointed dart had sunk into his flesh. Head sunk on his chest, he strained to heave the last bushel onto the wagon, then urged the team towards home.

Felicity's contemptuous barb had gone deep. Peter's mouth worked and his Adam's apple quivered, and he barely managed to keep his face rigid until he gained the privacy of the stable. There, he gave up on self-control and sank down on a bale of hay. On top of all his other troubles, the remarks of high-and-mighty girls seemed just too much for a fellow to bear. All by itself, Peter's face twisted up and he burst into tears. There was no telling how many of them he might have shed had Alec King not come padding up behind him.

"I heard what they said in the orchard, Peter," Alec told him understandingly. "I know it might be difficult, but, ah...don't let them see they can get your goat, hmm?"

This piece of bluff, manly advice stopped Peter's sobbing but he started sneezing instead. In spite of the day being cool, tiny beads of perspiration had popped up on his forehead. His cheeks, under their tan, displayed a pallor that made Alec frown.

"Are you all right there, lad?"

"I'm fine," Peter answered, in a voice so low and muffled that Alec walked round to get a good look at Peter in the light streaming through the stable window.

"You look pale to me."

"No, I'm all right," Peter protested energetically, even though he was looking more chalky by the minute. His heart thumped inside him, for the more he sneezed, the more he sounded like Edward Ray.

Alec thought he knew the source of Peter's anxiety.

"Don't you fret about your job. Hetty, she's not gonna let you go. The bark is a lot worse than the bite, I'd say."

This extracted only a weak smile from Peter. He thought Hetty could bite pretty hard when she wanted to. Alec, reassured somewhat, stepped back over the straw and left Peter alone in the stable. Peter wiped his eyes, pushed himself to his feet and followed. There was still the team to unharness and a whole wagon full of apples to unload.

The next morning, Hetty, Sara and Peter sat at breakfast while Olivia finished grilling some toast at the stove behind them. Sara ate silently while Peter merely toyed with his food. This was such odd behavior for both children that Hetty noticed right away.

"Cat got your tongue, Sara?"

"I just don't feel like talking," Sara replied. Though she usually kept everyone at Rose Cottage amused with a steady stream of stories and conversation, there were times when all Sara wanted to do was sit quietly with her own thoughts. Today she was troubled by what Felicity had said in the orchard, and Peter's low spirits reinforced Sara's suspicion that Felicity had truly hurt his feelings.

Olivia, who had just cooked up a delicious breakfast and dished it out generously, watched Peter. Peter usually did full justice to anything Olivia put in front of him.

"Is something wrong with your food, Peter?"

"No, the food's fine, Miss Olivia."

Nevertheless, Peter didn't make a move to eat anything. Since growing boys were usually hungry enough to eat the wood off a door frame, Olivia peered at Peter more closely.

"Why, Peter, you're perspiring. Are you ill?"

"He's probably just exhausted," Hetty remarked tartly. "I told you it was too much for him."

Peter blanched. Hetty must have seen how slowly he had unloaded the apples from the wagon yesterday. Before he even had time to duck, Olivia pressed a hand to Peter's forehead. Her eyebrows shot up in surprise.

"Oh, no, Hetty. He's burning up."

Hetty didn't approve of sickness in her household. She got up immediately and felt Peter's forehead for herself. Sara looked on, worried.

"Open your mouth, boy," Hetty commanded.

Not daring to do otherwise, Peter leaned his head back and gave Hetty a gaping view of his tonsils. Picking up a bread knife, Hetty depressed his tongue.

"Hmm, raw as calves' liver. Mix up some hot brine and ginger for him to gargle with, Olivia."

Sara felt that if there were any nursing to be done, she ought to be in on it. She hopped up from her chair.

"I'll put the kettle on."

Olivia stood gnawing her lip for a moment. She had less than perfect faith in hot brine and ginger.

"Hetty, I think I had better go for the doctor."

For just the merest fraction, Hetty looked about to argue. Then she saw the frank unease in Olivia's eyes and nodded her approval. As Olivia sped out, Peter began sweating twice as much as he had only minutes before. As if he weren't already warm enough, Hetty buttoned up his shirt and ordered him into the back bedroom just behind the kitchen, where anyone sick was put to be nursed.

Outside the King farm, Felicity pushed Cecily in the backyard swing while Felix idly tossed stones at a fencepost. News traveled fast in the King clan, and the children had already learned of Peter's condition from Olivia as she passed by on her way to fetch the doctor.

"I just know Peter's not sick," Felicity declared, giving Cecily a mighty shove.

"Just lazy," Felix agreed. He hadn't forgotten all the wood he had piled, just so that Peter could play. Just look where that bit of effort had led!

The only one who disagreed was Cecily. "Peter's not lazy!" she cried as the swing came swishing backward. Peter had always been nice to her, and she didn't know why he should be called names.

Felix made a face at Cecily, and would have made another, save for the approach of his mother. With one hand around Sara's shoulders and the other gripping Sara's suitcase, Janet King motioned her children to gather round. They trotted over quickly. When their mother frowned like that, she meant business.

"Children, listen to me, please. I don't want you to go anywhere near Peter for a while. He's seriously ill with the flu, and he's contagious. In the meantime, Sara's going to stay with us."

These instructions issued, Janet King trudged into the house with the suitcase, leaving Sara outside. Cecily, whose faith in Peter had been vindicated, now looked as though she wished Peter had merely been lazy. Felix turned to Sara with some alarm. Girls who came from infectious houses could very well be carrying some highly unpleasant disease.

"You're still feeling all right, aren't you, Sara?" he asked, half afraid for Sara, and half worrying about being laid out, green and queasy, himself.

"Of course I am," Sara retorted, realizing that Felix expected her to break out in spots before his very eyes.

"I hope we all don't get the flu now," grumbled Felicity. "Fancy getting the flu from a hired boy."

Perhaps there ought to have been two different kinds of flu, one for hired boys, and one, a much nicer one, for their employers. Sara turned on Felicity fiercely. She was the one who had seen

Peter collapse into bed, too weak even to lift this head.

"Felicity King, you bite your tongue! How dare you speak that way about Peter when he's sick."

Tossing her blond curls, Sara marched off toward the house after her Aunt Janet, quite pointedly leaving Felicity behind.

Sara was right to worry. Back at Rose Cottage, Hetty and Olivia followed Dr. Blair outside, and stood by while he climbed up into his buggy.

"Yes, but it was so sudden," Hetty was saying, as if amazed that any illness dared push its way so rudely into the ordered confines of Rose Cottage.

Dr. Blair stowed his black bag in the back and sighed. He was a grizzled fellow and had seen this sort of thing before. Though he had come as quickly as he could, and worked hard over Peter, the future didn't look hopeful.

"This is a bad case of virulent influenza. He's a very, very sick boy. I can't seem to get his fever down."

Olivia, ever determined to be optimistic, asked the bravest question. "But he will get better, won't he, Doctor?"

Dr. Blair avoided her eyes and picked up the reins. "I can't promise you that. The next twenty-four hours will be critical. He could go either way."

Matters were getting very serious, even for hired boys. Hetty put one hand to her mouth, as if finally realizing it.

"Oh lord, but—but there must be something we can do."

Hetty was a woman of action and command. If only there were one or two firm measures she could take, she felt she could have that flu on the run before the day was out.

Dr. Blair only shook his head. "No, I'm afraid not. Just keep giving him fluids. And," the doctor paused, then decided he'd better come out with the rest of what was on his mind, "you'd best send for his mother."

Chapter Eleven

At school the next day, Sara and Felicity wandered through the groups of playing children in the schoolyard. Sara was sunk in gloom. Felicity remained equally silent. Peter's condition occupied their thoughts completely. Since Peter's flu had become a life and death situation, Felicity had sobered considerably—but not to the extent that she didn't brighten up in a flash at the sight of Edward Ray approaching. Breaking away from Sara, Felicity ran toward him.

"Edward! Edward, you're back!"

"He's been up and around for nearly two days now," Clemmie announced proudly, bringing up the rear. Clemmie was quite intoxicated with the feeling of importance she had gained, helping her mother during the time Edward lay ill. Now, she meant to stick close to Edward all day and continue to harvest as much importance as possible.

"I was so sick, I almost died," Edward swiftly informed his companions as they all walked toward the school door. What good was a brush with death if a fellow couldn't use it later to impress a girl like Felicity?

"Guess what? Peter's sick now," Felicity told him, growing somber again. Like it or not, she was acquiring a painful respect for the kind of flu hired boys got.

"Very, very sick," Sara added. "The doctor's not sure he'll get better, either."

Felicity was so taken up with the shocking new realities that had entered her life, that the happy shouts of the schoolyard seemed a million miles away. She bit her lower lip.

"I don't believe it. I mean, babies die, old people die, but not people our age."

"He's got virulent influenza," Sara cautioned ominously.

Edward suddenly stopped cold in his tracks.

"I know how he got it—from me. And do you know what he did after I was so mean to him? He brought me medicine from your Aunt Hetty. Hasn't she given him any?"

"What medicine?" Felicity wanted to know—and she wanted to know rather urgently.

"Aunt Hetty never sent you any medicine," Sara cut in. Aunt Hetty would certainly have let the whole world know, had she been able to provide some miraculous cure for Edward Ray.

Edward frowned, trying to remember. Being half delirious with flu mixed things up so in a fellow's mind.

"The day the missionary spoke!" he said, hitting upon it.

"No."

Sara felt she was in a position to know everything that went on at Rose Cottage. And she certainly hadn't seen Aunt Hetty sending out anything to the Rays.

"But I'm sure Peter brought medicine," Edward insisted. After all, he'd been sitting right there in the kitchen, wretchedly inhaling steam, when Peter had knocked at the door. His mother had been mighty grateful for the delivery, too, and had made Edward drink cup after cup of the strange-tasting tea.

Sara's eyes suddenly grew wide. Besides Dr. Blair, there was only one other person in Avonlea from whom remedies could be gotten—that is, if people had the nerve to seek them out. And it was just that person Sara had seen with Peter on the day Edward fell ill.

"Maybe it was Peg Bowen!"

With Peter so desperately sick, Sara was desperate to help him get better. She would not leave any possibility untried. Although she had lived in the village quite long enough to have heard all the scary rumors about the witch of Avonlea, she'd also heard that Peg Bowen's remedies helped people get well.

She proposed an expedition to Peg's cabin for that very day, to leave right after school. Felicity and Felix would have nothing to do with such a dangerous mission, and raced home the minute school was over. But, much to Sara's surprise, Edward Ray volunteered to go with her. If Peg had had anything to do with his getting better, Edward wanted to know. Clemmie came along too. Even a trip to a witch's cabin with her fearless brother seemed less terrifying than walking all the way home alone.

Sara had been to Peg's cabin once before, and knew how to find it. Apprehensively, the three picked their way through the woods until it came into sight. The cabin lived up to all their expectations. Not only did it have a great black cauldron outside, simmering over a wood fire, but there were cats curled up in all the warm spots around it. A person couldn't really be a witch without her animal friends to keep her company.

"Look at those cats," Edward said nervously, as if he expected them all to suddenly take exception to his presence. Edward much preferred dogs when he had a choice.

Clemmie crowded close to her brother. She would have clutched his arm tightly had she dared.

"That mean one must be Peg Bowen," Clemmie whispered. "Ma says she can turn herself into a cat."

Clemmie was young enough to believe that if her mother said a thing, it really must be so. The cat accused of being mean lifted its orange head reproachfully. It had had to fend for itself in the woods before Peg took it in. It couldn't help it if its ears had been nipped ragged by frostbite.

"That's ridiculous," Sara shot back at Clemmie, feeling her palms go damp nonetheless. "I'm not afraid of her."

Now that she had announced that she wasn't afraid, Sara found it was up to her to prove it. Clemmie and Edward fell in behind her, leaving Sara to make the first move. Swallowing hard, Sara edged forward towards the cabin door. Just as she was about to knock, Peg Bowen herself suddenly stepped out behind them.

"What do you want?"

Clemmie, Edward and Sara all shrieked in unison. None of them had seen Peg, and they jumped as though she had just materialized out of thin air. It was very late in the day, and the dappled shade cast eerie shadows over Peg's face. All around, the trees whispered and sighed mysteriously. Clemmie grabbed Edward's sleeve and screwed up her eyes tight, certain that she was, even then, being turned into a beetle.

Peg seemed used to shrieking children for she just put one hand on her hip and looked Edward up and down.

"Edward, I see my potions had an effect on you."

So it *was* Peg who sent the precious medicine. Sara felt a leap of hope inside her, and Clemmie opened her eyes again.

"Your medicine saved my life," Edward admitted when he finally found his voice again. "Now it's Peter who's sick."

"Peter Craig?"

The mild amusement she had felt at the children's fright fled from Peg's sun-browned face and was instantly replaced by concern. Keenly, she scanned the faces of the children and saw from their taut expressions that the situation was serious indeed, and called for action.

Without another word, Peg tramped into her cabin and went to work. The children, not quite daring to follow, peeped in the door. There they saw an interior that didn't seem much different from the outdoors, for it smelled of the forest and was festooned all round with bunches of herbs hung upside down to dry. As Sara's eyes adjusted to the darkness, she spotted some of Peg's strange treasures: a stuffed monkey, a skull and a crow perched on the windowsill. Inside of a few minutes, Peg had put together a great handful of herbs and rolled them up inside a little cloth packet just like the one that had gone to Mrs. Ray.

Peg set out, with the children trotting behind

her. Very shortly, they arrived in the vicinity of Rose Cottage. Here, Peg dropped to the rear and handed Edward the packet.

"Here, you take it."

Once upon a time, many, many years ago, witches used to get a lot of respect. Indeed, they were often considered the wisest people around, for they knew all about herbs and healing teas and had memorized all the cures that got passed down from generation to generation when people had to look out for themselves. They could fix up a raging infection or mix a potion to help a broken heart. People traveled long distances just to ask them about important things. Oh, it used to be a very grand thing to be a witch.

But being a witch had become a pretty suspect business in Peg's time—especially in a place like Avonlea. This was why she had to give her medicine and her instructions to Edward to take to the Rose Cottage door.

Edward went up the steps and knocked smartly. Hetty opened it, looking quite as frazzled as Mrs. Ray had previously, and more than a little surprised to see Edward standing there.

"Why, Edward. Yes?"

Edward held out his gift.

"I brought some medicine for Peter, Miss Hetty."

Hetty looked at the little packet in puzzlement and automatic suspicion. Edward Ray didn't exactly seem a likely source of flu cures.

"I don't understand."

"I would have died if Peter hadn't brought it for me. It's an herb mixture from Peg Bowen."

Considering the hot exchange Hetty had had with Peg in church, perhaps Edward oughtn't to have let that slip. Hetty snapped straight as a poker.

"Peg Bowen?"

Nodding, Edward glanced back at the others. Determinedly, he thrust the packet into Hetty's hand.

"You're to put these in a quart of water, boil them up and give him a cup every half hour or so."

Slowly, Hetty closed her fingers over the herbs, in spite of their having come from Peg Bowen. Truth to tell, Hetty was at her wits' end about Peter. She was willing to try just about anything, including Peg's wild brew, if it would turn back Peter's raging fever.

"Thank you, Edward," she said uncertainly.

Hetty was holding onto the remedy so gingerly that Edward suddenly felt the need of some major added reinforcement to make sure she used it. Besides, his conscience had been weighing on him like a boulder ever since his recovery, and he felt he simply had to relieve it.

"Miss Hetty, I'm the one who let your horse run away with the buggy. Peter got all the blame, but it was really my fault."

As Edward dashed down the steps to the other children, Hetty still stood in the door, quite bewildered. The last thing on her mind, right then, was runaway horses, and Edward's confession had taken her completely by surprise.

Just then, Hetty caught sight of Peg Bowen. Perhaps the memory of that day in church surfaced in Hetty's mind, for she suddenly flushed red. Now here was the very same Peg Bowen giving her something to help Peter. Hetty hesitated, then waved.

"Peg!"

Peg was taking no chances with Hetty King. If either of them started talking, who knew what sort of fireworks might erupt. Peg slipped out of sight as swiftly and easily as a fox on the run.

"Peg, come back!" Hetty called out, but it was no use. When Peg made up her mind to disappear, no one could make her show herself again.

Hetty stepped out onto the porch and looked about in vain. Then, with a shake of her head, she patted the herb packet, smiled faintly and went back inside to get straight to work on Peter.

Chapter Twelve

Dr. Blair returned that day to take another look at his patient. He took Peter's pulse and felt his forehead. Olivia stood by the side of the bed along with Peter's mother, Mrs. Craig. Mrs. Craig had dropped old Mrs. Connolly's laundry straight back into the washtub when she heard of her son's illness. She hadn't known what to expect, but what she found at Rose Cottage exceeded her worst imaginings. Now she wrung her hands as she watched the doctor, her care-worn face one tremendous knot of worry. She had just that moment rushed into the back bed-room, her hat and coat still on.

"His pulse is weaker." The doctor grimaced. He spoke in a very low voice, but his words pierced every bosom nonetheless.

Peter lay pale and seemingly unconscious under the quilt. Endless beads of perspiration dotted his forehead. His breath was shallow and frighteningly faint. Olivia stepped softly to the bed and bent over Peter, speaking close to his ear so he could hear.

"Peter, dear, your mother's here."

Mrs. Craig sank down on the bed, immediately picking up Peter's hand. She was trying very hard to keep her own from shaking.

"Peter? Peter, I'm here. You're going to be all right."

Slowly, very slowly, Peter's eyes eased open, but they seemed to have difficulty focusing on anything. His mother picked up a nearby cloth and began to wipe his forehead, for having infectious influenza was a very hot, damp, uncomfortable business indeed.

"Mama?" Peter's voice was a mere thread, incredulous and raspy.

"Mm-hm."

Mrs. Craig made a soft, reassuring sound in the back of her throat, just like a mother cat greeting her only kitten. Peter's lashes fluttered shut, then open again. He was having a hard time grasping that the person he had been dreaming about so much was actually here. Reality was all mixed up with delusions in his fevered mind.

"How did you get here? Did Papa bring you?"

Olivia and the doctor looked away. Mrs. Craig swallowed hard and squeezed her son's fingers.

"Papa's gone away, remember? He will come back...as soon as he can."

As if remembering the sad facts, Peter's head rolled sideways a little on the pillow. His eyes shut again and stayed shut, causing his mother to blanch with dread.

"Peter? You mustn't go to sleep, Peter. You've got to fight."

The battle had reached a critical stage, and a lot depended on Peter's own will to survive. Hetty, who had just come into the room, saw at once how deeply distressed Mrs. Craig really was, no matter how hard the woman was trying to hide it. Quickly, Hetty touched Olivia's shoulder and motioned towards the door. Olivia followed and Hetty shut the door behind them. What the sick boy needed above all was his own mother. But maybe there *was* something Hetty could do. She put a pot of water on the stove and, with a word to Dr. Blair, began to brew Peg's herb remedy.

Outside Rose Cottage, the three King children, along with Sara and Edward sat down on the porch steps. They had seen the doctor come and go, and heard the grown-ups' whispers. Although no one would tell them, they knew that Peter was worse.

"Poor Peter," Cecily sighed. Her lower lip

began to quiver as she remembered how Peter always had a grin for her, no matter how hard he had been working. He would toss her an apple from the wagon too, so that she didn't have to go to the orchard to pick one for herself.

Felix also had apparently been searching his conscience and not liking what he found.

"We've been so mean to him, and he's never done anything to any of us."

"He's twice as smart as a lot of boys," Edward admitted, almost, but not quite, yielding his position as the brightest boy in school.

"And a much harder worker," Felix conceded in an absolute fit of generosity. Since Felix generally avoided hard work himself, he had all the more cause to admire it in others.

Tears had begun to brim in Sara's eyes, and she had to blink very hard to keep them from spilling over completely. She kicked one of her heels against the lowest step.

"It's too late to be saying all this. Peter will never know how much we thought of him."

"Maybe he will get better," Edward said bravely.

Cecily twisted at her cuff and furrowed her young brow. She had just thought of something else.

"If Peter does die, will he go to Heaven, even if he's not a Presbyterian?"

"I don't want him to go to Heaven or anywhere else," Sara burst out passionately. "I just want him to stay here."

At this point, Sara's eyes did brim over with tears. Even Felicity wavered on the verge of crying. Just before the first sniffle got out, she took hold of herself and managed to remain dry-eyed. Her expression grew steadily sadder, though, as if she were remembering how Peter had always admired her and how happy it had made him once just to catch hold of her hand. In fact, it was a bit of a shock for all the children to discover how much they really liked and cared about Peter. Hired boys were exactly like any other kind of boys, with personalities, and feelings, and mothers who cared desperately about them.

That night, nobody went to bed in the King household. There seemed no point, for not one of them would have been able to sleep for worry about what was happening in Rose Cottage. Instead, they sat up in the kitchen, shrouded in silent gloom, dozing off around the big, comfortingly warm wood stove. Sara, who had been sent to stay with her cousins in case she might catch Peter's flu, was curled up in the old rocking chair. Slowly, she started to slide sideways and then came awake with a start. Blinking, she rubbed her eyes and stared out the kitchen window, surprised that the night had passed and she was looking into a soft, pink dawn.

Sara blinked again, then sat bolt upright so suddenly that the rocking chair nearly tipped on its rockers. A slender figure wrapped in a shawl was hurrying up the lane outside.

"Someone's coming. It's Aunt Olivia!"

Before Sara could even jump up, Olivia rushed into the kitchen. Her hair was untidy, her hat askew and her eyes ringed with smudgy circles from lack of sleep. Through all this haggardness, Olivia was quite radiant.

"His fever's broken. He's out of danger," she cried triumphantly, all but tripping over the rag rug in her excitement.

Everyone had been so afraid of the worst that it took a good half a minute for the news to sink in. Then joy flooded the household. Felicity looked as though a ten-ton weight had been lifted from her. Sara broke into a gigantic smile. Aunt Janet rose up out of the old corner armchair in relief.

"Oh, thank God."

Her gaze swept over her own brood, glad and thankful that the influenza wasn't going to run rampant there. Uncle Alec, who had Felix cradled in his lap, caught her look and smiled back in perfect understanding.

"Peter's going to be all right," he murmured to Felix as he shifted the boy's sleepy head.

Chapter Thirteen

Once over the crisis, Peter mended rapidly. It wasn't long at all before he was able to sit up in bed and put away a good helping of Hetty's chicken soup. Hetty took pride in her soup and was a great believer in its nourishing powers. She stood at the foot of the bed folding a blanket and watching Peter eat. Mrs. Craig sat next to Peter with her arm around him. She didn't care about eating or sleeping or anything else except that Peter was getting better. She might be a poor woman, reduced to working as a housekeeper, but at that moment she looked happier than any millionaire.

"You're all I have in the world," Mrs. Craig said fondly to Peter. "I wish I could look after you myself."

When it came to looking after people, Hetty considered herself an expert. Hadn't she taken in Sara and swept all the fancy Montreal notions clean out of her head?

"You're not to worry, Maude Craig. We will take good care of him here. I'll make sure he doesn't go to work till he's good and ready. Oh, with winter coming on, there won't be so much work to be done."

With the matter settled as far as she was concerned, Hetty left the room, the blanket tucked under her arm. Peter swallowed down the last delicious mouthful of soup and looked up at his mother. She'd been through a dreadful ordeal in the last few days and he didn't want her to worry any more.

"I'll be fine, Mama. I'll stay here till Papa comes back, like we planned."

Mrs. Craig smiled and gave him a pat just to show him what a good, brave boy he had turned out to be. As she did so, the door opened a crack and Felix peeped in. Mrs. Craig spied him and winked.

"You have visitors," she told her son.

Peter set down the empty soup bowl and looked up with surprise and pleasure. His mother left, carrying the bowl with her, meaning to give

Peter some time with his friends. Felix, followed by all the other children, slipped into the room and gathered around Peter's bed. They had all waited anxiously for this moment and found themselves in a strongly confessional mood.

"Peter," Sara began, "I'm sorry I made you go to church with us. Look at all the trouble I've caused."

Exactly what trouble she had caused wasn't clear in Sara's mind, but she was sure she must be responsible for a load of it. Perhaps if she had let Peter take up Methodism, he wouldn't have been struck down in his tracks.

As for Peter, it was quite a new and heady experience to have all the King clan, as well as Edward and Clemmie Ray, gathered breathlessly about him. It made him positively expansive.

"That's all right," Peter said generously to Sara. "To tell you the truth, I quite liked church."

He didn't have a chance to say exactly what it was he liked about it, for Felicity, to his utter astonishment, broke openly into a sob.

"Oh, Peter, I'm so sorry I acted the way I did."

She did have quite a bit to be sorry for, but Peter would never have dreamed of pointing that out. Merely having Felicity actually shed a tear for him had Peter practically melted into a puddle. He didn't mind having the flu if this was the effect it had on girls he admired.

"That's all right, Felicity." His smile was so wide his face seemed in danger of splitting.

With quivering lips, Felicity smiled back—and Edward Ray didn't mind one bit. Now he, too, had been through the trial of infectious influenza, and the experience had pretty well wiped out his airs of superiority towards Peter.

"When you're all better, will you come fishing with me? I'll show you my best spot," he promised. Everyone knew this was a big offer, for Edward always boasted about the size of the fish he caught and kept the places where he caught them his private secret.

More tribute was flowing Peter's way than he knew what to do with. His brown eyes, no longer shy or wary, glowed with inner happiness. He didn't mind at all being the Kings' hired boy so long as he could also be their friend.

"Sure, Edward. Thanks."

When Peter was pronounced completely back to health, the occasion was celebrated with a picnic in the King orchard. Felix and his father had lugged out a picnic table, and it was now groaning under the weight of all sorts of delicious food. Cecily approached it importantly, carrying the biggest, most scrumptious marble cake Felicity had been able to bake. Peter had missed getting a taste at the church picnic. Felicity was determined he shouldn't miss such a spectacular treat again.

Behind Cecily, something of a ceremony was going on. Uncle Alec, in the hole that he and Felix had dug that morning, was carefully packing soil around a newly planted sapling. Hetty, Olivia, Peter and Mrs. Craig, all of them dressed grandly, approached through the orchard. Felix was the first to see them.

"They're coming," he called out excitedly.

Aunt Janet helped Cecily set the cake down in the place of honor and came round the table, wiping her hands on her apron.

"Oh, Peter," she exclaimed, "you've got a new suit. Don't you look handsome."

Peter had had a haircut, too, and looked quite the smart young gentleman. Either the Methodists *or* the Presbyterians would have been proud to have him.

Hetty King, who had provided the suit, nodded her head.

"Well, if he intends going to church with us this winter, he will need it...for warmth."

Sara saw right through her aunt's brisk practicality and gave Hetty a crushing bear hug. There would be no more prickly discussions with Peter about clothes.

"Oh, thank you, Aunt Hetty."

"Sara, don't make a spectacle of yourself," Hetty admonished hastily, flustered by the demonstration.

Uncle Alec came and saved her with a gesture beckoning everyone to gather round.

"Now, before we eat, there's one thing we must do. Sara..."

Sara answered the cue and stepped over to the tremulous little sapling. To announce her, Felix put his hands to his mouth and mimicked a trumpet blast. Nobody even minded that he sounded much more like a moose with a head cold than a musical instrument. Cecily and Felix took Peter by the arms and led him over to the freshly planted apple tree. Sara cleared her throat. She was famous for her dramatic recitations and had been unanimously chosen to make the speech.

"We dedicate this tree in the famous King orchard to Peter Craig, in hope that he may lead a long and happy life with us here at the King farm."

If Sara had expected some reply from Peter, she would have waited a very long time, for Peter was completely overcome. He stood staring at the tree and staring at the Kings and turning every color of the rainbow. In spite of all the attention he had received, he couldn't believe that people as important as the Kings would do such a thing just for him. He gazed joyfully at the tree and wished Peg Bowen could have been there.

Beside him, his mother wasn't in much better condition. She had to whip out her handkerchief and dab at her eyes, speechless that people should be so kind to her son. Felicity smiled at Peter which, as far as Peter was concerned, was almost as good as having another tree planted. Even Hetty's throat worked suspiciously—a signal to Uncle Alec that he had better do something fast before the whole crowd burst out into fountains of happy tears.

"Hooray!" he shouted enthusiastically.

At that, everyone started applauding and the sobs were safely averted. As for Peter, he still couldn't say a word, but he made up for it with smiles and brilliant scarlet ears. At last Peter Craig, hired boy, really belonged somewhere.